Home Sweet Road

Anthony St. Clair

rucksack
universe

Rucksack Press
Eugene, Oregon

CONTENTS

"The hills of the Twelve Bens whisper long-lost secrets that pass through the town of Clifden and sail their dreams and messages across the Atlantic Ocean to the rest of the world. Located at Ireland's western edge, Clifden is the unofficial capital of Connemara. A little over an hour's drive from New Galway, on your way you'll meander through scenic boglands, and you can visit The Blast Memorial in the ruins of Galway. An Irish legend speaks of great power and otherworldly beings in Clifden, but today's globetrotter comes to hike the Twelve Bens and to enjoy the hospitality of the Eighth Wonder of the World Hostel. Be sure to visit The Salt and Crane for an Irish breakfast, the best pint of Galway Pradesh Stout west of Dublin, and the daily (and nightly) live music sessions."

— Guru Deep, *Ireland Through the Third Eye*

I

THE DAY THE MOUNTAIN ARRIVED in the hills, the Awen of Ireland skipped her usual hostel chores and checked the floor, the wall, and the rock.

Satisfied that all was in order and everything was still where it was supposed to be hidden, Aisling left the rock and started back toward the hostel. The morning mists swirled around her in the soft light, and she felt the dampness in the curls of her hair, red as Australia's Uluru and curly as the bends in a Himalayan road. West and in front of her, the small town of Clifden, Ireland, nestled in the hills. Aisling breathed in the air, salty from the sea and peaty from the bog where she was walking, and she listened to what it told her. The air and the earth told her the same thing, and so did the ocean on the breeze and the mists drizzling from the clouds.

They're coming. They're coming.

Once she had walked far enough, Aisling turned around, putting Clifden to her back. She stared east at the Twelve Bens, the dozen hills that sold the postcards at her front desk and filled the beds of her hostel. Curious travelers would drink cheap wine in the front room and read from their Guru Deep *Ireland Through the Third Eye* guidebooks, and they would talk about the Bens. Full of a mystical power, it was said. Something otherworldly. Something beyond imagination.

Or so the legends say, Aisling thought with a grin, *but at least I know the truth.*

She heard it again: *They're coming. They're coming.*

Not that she needed to, but she counted. The Twelve Bens themselves were as unchanged as ever, but a thirteenth hill now stood behind them. The shock still buzzed through her though, as sharp as when she had first gotten out of bed and looked out her window at the hills like she always did.

This is a lot to take in before a cuppa tea.

People loved Clifden and they loved the Twelve Bens. They came from all the world over, usually stopping first at The Blast Memorial where Galway used to be, then catching a bus in New Galway and heading north, where the hills were brown and green, where the peat was in the earth and in the air. Despite all the soft rain that made the place feel quiet and remote, the world crackled with energy here, the travelers liked to say. Some people claimed it was a residual explosive power from The Blast, but the researchers at the center near the Memorial had disproven that time and time again. Besides, they said, nothing was lingering now, nearly two centuries later.

The mountain looked nothing like the hills. It was as if one of the Himalayas had hitchhiked from Asia to Ireland, stopping just short of the Atlantic. Aisling had never seen anything like the mountain, not in all her days in Clifden as a girl growing up, not in all her days traveling the world, and certainly not since she had returned. As a child she had seen pictures of the Himalayas, and as a woman she had seen them with her own eyes, felt them with her hands and feet, breathed their thin, impossible air. The soft, green-brown hills of the Twelve Bens rolled like waves, slowly rising and falling through the eons. But the mountain behind them stood gray, brown, and white. There was no gentle rolling to it, only sharp angles that grew and grew and grew and would never stop rising unless the world itself ceased to be.

"Why are you here?" Aisling said.

As she stared, she had a feeling the mountain was silent only because it didn't want to say anything yet.

Staring at the mountain, the dream returned. A woman stood in a mountain's shadow. Aisling could not see her face, but she could see glints of blue and green, as if the woman wore a necklace with a pendant made from a brilliant gem. The gleam vanished, and the fear in the woman's wail had made Aisling wake in a sweat, her heart pounding.

Aisling returned to the Eighth Wonder of the World, opening the hostel's front door and soaking in the dry warmth of the fire she'd set in the front room stove before leaving. *All the scent of peat without the damp, plus warmth,* she thought, going behind the front desk to fix a cuppa tea. The sight of the mountain, so jarring, and the first thing she'd done had been to make sure that the three were undisturbed. *No breakfast, no tea—at least I got dressed. But if this means the test has come...*

"Naw, it's true," came a male voice from the front room across from the desk. Aisling stirred her tea, which was dark as peat and strong as a proper pint of Galway Pradesh Stout. She couldn't see the two travelers, so they had to be sitting at the table in the left corner, out of sight from the desk. "That bloke," the man continued, "he managed to get five hitchhikers in the same car, including himself. No one knew how, not even the other hitchhikers, but I saw them get out of the car, packs and all."

"Well," said another man, his voice deeper, "why

didn't you ask him how he did it?"

"Ask him? Well, I... I couldn't, mate, just couldn't."

"What's wrong with you? Fancy him so much that your pack got your tongue?"

"Not that. Not that at all. You know my eye don't wander."

"Much."

"Well, okay. Eyes yes, hands no. But that's not the point. Point is, he done it. And when he got out of the car, he just... he just looked at me, these eyes like a grassy field at noon. Never seen eyes like 'em. I couldn't talk."

"Never knew you to be so love-struck."

"Only when I look at you, mate. You know that. But then the other travelers, they walked by me as the one went the other way. And they were saying, 'Yeah, mate. That's him, the one who stopped that raging elephant with nothing but a bandanna and an empty beer can. Nothing stops that bloke. He goes everywhere. He could go up a mountain and back in a day, I tell you.'"

Aisling sipped her tea.

Another story.

She hadn't paid the stories much mind at first, especially three years ago, when she was just settling into her new role. Travelers always told tall tales, but soon enough she was paying close attention. The stories had been trickling in more and more lately. Always the same man. Always the same impossible circumstances. But there had to be something to them.

This was the third time and the third accent she'd heard about the hitchhikers, and the fifth time she'd heard about the elephant. Sometimes it was a beer bottle, not a beer can. Other than that, the details didn't change much, but more and more stories kept trickling into Clifden.

Travelers spoke of a lanky, grubby backpacker who had rescued kids from pirates using nothing but a joke and a bottle of rum. One night over pints, Aisling had heard the one about a prime minister, new laws, and an end to corruption. Then there were the ten tellings of the same traveler crossing borders with nothing but a wink, not even a passport—or a pocket to put one in. How many people had gone through a border crossing naked and made it to the next country on the other side?

Sometimes the details were murky, but even in western Ireland, in Connemara, in wee Clifden, at the edge of the world, the tales of the traveler came.

Aisling sipped more tea. *I wonder if I'll ever get to meet him,* she thought. *Maybe he'd be someone who I could—*

She shook her head. Better not to think about it. Solitude. She'd expected solitude, welcomed it even, when she took on not the job, but the life.

Aisling touched the desk, and the breath of the world rippled into her through the wood. No one had said anything about being lonely. It wasn't a requirement. It had simply become a circumstance.

Sometimes, the loneliness burned through her, and it burned through her now. She finished the tea, ate a light breakfast, and tended to such chores as she had to tend to that morning, as guests checked out or ate breakfast or presented questions about where to go and what to do today.

They all went on their way. *But not me, Aisling thought. All the wide world is stamped in the little passport in my nightstand, but I'll never leave Clifden again.*

The hostel was quiet, and she had a hunch the day would remain quiet. She left a sign on the desk for guests to check themselves in and to direct inquiries to The Salt and Crane.

She stopped in her room and slung the case over her shoulder.

Lonely or not, I am who I am, she thought. I can't help that I've never found a man here interesting, either local or traveler. I'm just... They're just too different. Or I'm too much myself. Plus, well, the other thing, and that makes me too different. I don't know anymore.

The loneliness started to feel heavy as a sweater in the rain.

She pulled the front door closed behind her. *Bugger this, she thought. I'm getting a pint.*

And I need to talk to Connemara anyway.

Aisling set off toward the Clifden city center. A

weak sun glowed through the thinning clouds and fading mist. She pushed down at the loneliness. Her thoughts kept turning to the world beyond her duty, to the mountain in the hills, to the black decimation that used to be Galway, once the gem of Ireland. Above all, she kept thinking of the three things hidden beneath the floor, behind the wall, and inside the rock—and how afraid she kept feeling that the test she had long dreaded was upon her at last.

THE HARDEST PART was never the playing. It was forgetting you had an audience.

Between tunes, Aisling picked up her pint glass and took a long draw of Galway Pradesh Stout. Aisling had drunk it the world over, but it never tasted as good as it did at home. The original Galway brewery might have been lost in The Blast, but fortunately there had been a backup location in the wee village that later grew to become New Galway.

Fortified, she raised her fiddle and bow again. A deep breath pulled the music from out of the air. In the moment her eyes were closed, all the people in the packed pub vanished from her thoughts. Aisling started a three-tune set: the ever-changing, fast-paced "The White Sign," the bouncy, playful "Connor in the Wheelbarrow," and the strange, jarring surprise of "Basket of Glass." All local favorites. All tunes she'd played for the men and women of Clifden since she was a girl.

The music faded. Applause took its place.

Then she saw the travelers and nearly dropped her fiddle.

The two men's green-gold eyes shone bright as a summer field at noon. They could have been brothers, but not Irish ones. Those deep tans weren't local.

One of the pub's old-time regulars walked over, stout sloshing out of his pint glass "What are you playing next, Aisling?" he asked, blocking her view.

"Taking a breather," she replied.

"When you get back, how about 'Wizard Walk?'"

"'The White Sign' wasn't enough?"

"Ah, but you know they go together." Mischief played at his brown-black eyes. "And 'The Traveler' makes a fine third."

Aisling glanced over at the men. *Indeed.*

"All right," she said. "I'll play both. But I've already done 'The White Sign,' so you think of a good third tune while I get some refreshment."

Deep in thought, the old man drained his beer as Aisling walked to the bar. *Come on,* she thought as she glared at the bartender. *I came in early so's to have a word. Didn't think I'd have to be here all day for it.*

The bartender glanced around the pub and shrugged. Aisling understood: the crowd stayed thirsty, and GPS took ages to pour. "Another stout?" the bartender asked.

"Aye, Jake." She glanced at the two men, standing near her at the bar. One of them stiffened, and a shadow seemed to pass over his eyes. The other man chuckled.

"What's so funny?" she asked. There was something about this one too. He was not the same, not as intense, but still—wow, the two of them...

The other man shrugged. "Seems like everywhere I go, the bartender is named Jake."

"You'd think they'd be more creative," said the first man, the shadow still hard and dark over his eyes.

"Just a name," the other man said.

"Think what you want."

"What's your deal?" The other man nodded to Jake and picked up a pint glass, brimming full of black stout and topped with a creamy white head. "He's still gotten our beers."

"And you'll find no finer anywhere," Aisling said. "That's from right down the road, you know, from New Galway. Fresh as morning mist."

"I suppose that will do," the first man said, making no move to pick up the unclaimed full pint. He just stared at Aisling, but the shadow lifted from his eyes.

If this is what it feels like just to look at each other, she thought, *what would it feel like—*

"Must've been something I ate," the first man said. "I don't think I can do the pint right now. Excuse me." He headed off toward the toilets.

"Sorry about that," the other man said, sticking out his hand. "Jay."

"It happens," she replied. "No worries." She shook Jay's hand, looking him in the eye. *This is near as bad as just watching the two of them*, she thought, hesitating before relinquishing the touch of his rough skin and strong yet gentle grasp. How the hell does a man have hands like that? You never get that around here. "My name's Aisling," she said.

"Ash-leeng," Jay replied, taking his time with each syllable. His voice had clearly come from America, but wherever Jay had traveled, his accent had taken souvenirs from every language and slang he'd encountered.

"A Yank who can pronounce my name correctly," she said, smiling. "I'm impressed. You'd be amazed how many Americans think my name is Ashley. Ashley. For feck's sake. Not hard at all, unless you're American, apparently." She grinned and tilted her head. "Present company excepted, of course."

"Glad I made the cut," Jay replied. "Makes me feel better. Tiran can be a bit brusque, and I can't say we're making the best impression for two blokes who just got to town." Jake set a brimming pint of GPS in front of Aisling. "Let me try to make up for it," Jay said, pulling money out of his pocket. "The pint's on me. Least I can do for the music."

The bartender shook his head. "The Awen's pints are always on the house," he said, smiling briefly at them both, then heading off again to pour more pints.

"The whaten? And why can I hear the capital A?"

Aisling shrugged and picked up the pint. "Don't know what you mean. Must have misheard him saying my name. Pubs are bugger noisy places, you know." *Dammit, Jake,* she thought. *You know we don't use the titles around the people. You certainly wouldn't like it if I referred to you as "the Jake," or spouted off about the other Jakes and Jades all over the bloody world.*

"I consider myself a bit of an expert."

"Really?" Aisling said. "You mean this isn't your first trip to Ireland? And here I was expecting the usual American vacationer come to ogle The Blast Memorial," she said. "Fair enough, though. Some say the country was headed for some sort of civil war, but all the death from The Blast put the Yanks off killing each other."

"We still have our flaws," Jay replied, "but I can't imagine what the country would've been like if that war had broken out." He took a draw off his pint. "Wow, that is the best pint of GPS I've ever had." He took another long quaff. "Actually, this is my first time in Ireland," he said.

"Ah, holiday. When do you need to be back to work in America?"

A shadow dropped over Jay's eyes. "Oh, no," he said. "If I'm on holiday, it's a lifelong one. I left the USA about three years ago. Been in Australia, been in Africa. Took my time, saw what I could on this go-around. Hitched up to Egypt near the end, left Cairo for Dublin after a stop in London on a freighter ship a few weeks back."

"Three years?" Aisling asked. Africa. Hitchhiking. The story she overheard earlier.

No, it couldn't be.

"Met Tiran on the Clifden bus leaving New Galway," Jay continued. "Turns out we'd both just come from The Blast Memorial. And good timing too. There was some sort of kerfuffle up there, I heard, as we were waiting."

"What happened?" Aisling asked, trying to keep her voice even.

"Someone going where they shouldn't be." Jay thought for a moment. "Maybe even a theft." He shrugged. "Well, I'm sure it's all sorted out by now. Security's pretty tight down there, after all."

Yes, Aisling thought, *it would be. Don't want people digging around the black ash that used to be Galway. Might be nearly two centuries later, but who knows what's left. Though Grandmother had some stories to tell. And goodness knows Connemara and I have seen some strange things when we've gone there in the night.*

"Sorry about that," the other man said with a honey rasp that made Aisling warm in bits that hadn't felt warm in a long time. "I seem to have lost my manners earlier," he said, standing between them and sticking out his hand. "Tiran."

"So I gathered," she said, smiling. "Aisling."

"Ah, a good Irish name," Tiran said. "Means 'dream' or 'vision,' if I remember correctly."

"Points for the other American," Aisling said, grinning, wondering if her gaze was indeed growing stupider and stupider as she stared at him. "It must be my lucky day. Two Yanks who can say my name. What's a girl to do?"

"What's a man to do?" Tiran replied. "I'm lucky I can speak at all, to look at you. No wonder the Irish don't mind the clouds. Your eyes are all the blue a man needs."

Aisling's reply vanished.

Jay seemed to be scowling, but he raised his glass and covered his mouth. When he lowered the empty pint he said, "Well, Tiran, maybe we should nip back to the hostel, finish getting settled in."

"Fair enough, lads," Aisling said. "I'm sure I'll see you there."

"You're staying there too?" Jay asked.

She laughed. "Of course. It's my hostel."

"We checked in already," Jay said.

"And now doubly so." She looked from Jay to Tiran and back again like a ship bouncing around stormy waves. "I'll be around to check you out, though. No worries."

The men went on their way. Aisling turned back to her pint, a good cover for staring down the bar to where Jake was topping up several pints of GPS.

When she looked up from her pint, Tiran was standing next to her. Beer slopped onto the bar.

"Sorry to startle you," Tiran said. "I had to come back. Told Jay I'd dropped my wallet."

"And did you?"

Tiran grinned as he tossed something onto the bar. "Apparently so."

Aisling grinned back.

"I had to ask you something," Tiran said, leaning in a little closer. "Would you care to meet me here later?"

Those eyes, she thought. *Those eyes*. "I'd love to. How about eight?"

Tiran nodded and his fingertips brushed her hand. "Gladly."

She watched him leave. Her fingers tightened as if squeezing something. When she looked down the bar again, Jake's scowl took the smile off her face as he came over.

"At last," she said. "Not busy for two seconds."

"It's one of those days," he said.

"At least the world is still turning."

Some of the people nursing their whiskeys went over to the musician's corner. They took out fiddles, flutes, and bodhráns. Soon notes, trills, and thumps filled the pub with music, a convenient camouflage for the Awen and the Jake.

"Do you know how hard it is to get these people to drink something other than stout?" Jake shook his head. "I should get a pay raise just for what it took to get some whiskeys on the bar. You just can't influence bloody stout. Stuff's so solid, so damn real you could stand a spoon in it. But there's a lot of folks in here whose lives needed a wee nudge."

"You made all these people start playing music so we wouldn't be overheard," Aisling said. "Who would've thought the Jake of Connemara would have things so hard?"

"Who would've thought the Awen of Ireland would blush like a schoolgirl with her first crush?"

"Why, Connemara," Aisling said, "are you jealous?"

Jake laughed. "You're practically my sister," he said. "Not jealous. Concerned. Did you hear what happened at The Blast Memorial earlier?"

"Jay mentioned something he overheard."

"He was right. Someone did get into one of the restricted areas, one where there was an excavation going on. Word is researchers were on the trail of some important relic, ancient and lost in The Blast, but it was always thought that the thing was powerful, important, and may give some sort of insight into what happened."

"All this time," said Aisling. "You'd think we'd at least know that by now."

"Whatever," Jake said. "I think that person wasn't there by chance. Somehow, he knew what was going on. I think he found the relic and stole it."

Aisling thought of her dream, the blue and green glints. "Does anyone know what it could have been?"

Jake shrugged. "There are stories of a powerful necklace, lost in The Blast, worn by a woman who came from the Heart of the World itself. But they're only stories. If that is what was stolen, though... From what I understand, the power that can be generated and focused through that necklace would bring the world to its knees."

"What? More than...?"

Jake nodded. "We know nothing yet though. All we can do is hope that's not what it was."

"Or that there isn't something worse that we don't know about."

"Cheerful Awen. Bloody cheerful you are sometimes."

"As if I didn't have enough to wonder about," Aisling said, then took another swig of stout. "Speaking of relics, I wanted to tell you that I checked them all this morning. Did you see what appeared in the Bens overnight?"

Jake sighed. After a moment, he nodded. "At least we're the only ones who can see it," he said, glancing around the pub, "but I don't understand it at all."

"Isn't that when you ask your Management for some insight?"

"The Management aren't saying anything about it. Which means one of two things. Either they don't know what the hell it is and they're biding their time until they know more, or they know exactly what's going on, but there's some larger damn destiny at work and they have to let things play out."

"Do you ever wonder what would happen if they were the ones living the lives, wondering where they were going, how they were going to make it day to day, putting themselves on the line, instead of being in whatever passes for an ivory tower when you're not exactly human?"

"I know you don't care for them," Jake said, "but I trust them."

"You work for them."

"I chose and was chosen," Jake replied. "Same as any of us. I'm here because I believe in them and in what we do. Whatever's happening, or whatever they're letting happen, it's for the right reasons. Even if we don't know them yet."

"Your faith is ever an example."

"And your surliness is unbecoming, little sister."

Aisling shook her head. "You're right," she replied. "It's just that—"

"It's just that you feel ever more lonely, and not one but two men blow in who both get under your skin like no man ever has."

"No one said being the Awen was easy. I just never expected to feel so set apart."

"No one ever said being a Jake or Jade was easy either. Being set apart doesn't necessarily get easier, but it becomes more tolerable when you stay focused on why you do what you do."

"Maybe I'm having trouble seeing that right now."

"Crap timing," Jake said. "Those two men did also just roll in from New Galway."

"And both said they had visited The Blast Memorial today. I know."

"Do you?"

She glared at him. "I have my duty, Connemara, same as you. And I'll do it."

"Your grandmother was Awen for decades. Seems every year someone showed up to test her, going for the relics. She'd barely been on the job a week when the first came. Three years you've been Awen, but you've never been tested."

"I hate that sometimes," Aisling said. "You look hardly older than me, but you're near as old as Grandmother was when she passed on."

"Perk of the job."

"You knew her far better than I ever did."

Jake shrugged. "I wish it could've been different, but it wasn't. She died before you came back, and you're the Awen of Ireland now," he said. "Muse.

Seer. Protector. As goes Ireland, so goes the world."

"I know good and well what my grandmother used to say."

"No, you don't," Jake replied. "You weren't even here when she died. You were off gallivanting the globe, remember?"

"Far too well. But I came back. And goodness knows you've been telling me everything Grandmother said to you ever since."

"No," Jake said. "Everything your grandmother said to *you*. She just knew she wouldn't be around to tell you herself, so she asked me to be her voice."

Aisling's hard gaze softened. "I didn't know that."

"But you're learning more and more, Awen," he said. "The relics are safe for now, but a threat came to Clifden today, Aisling. The time of your first test has come."

"You think it's Jay or Tiran?"

"I can't make sense of either of them. I can see the destinies and possibilities, the choices and consequences that flow out of most people. It's like rivers of lightning flowing out of everyone."

"That's one of the things about being a Jake, right? Part of how you know what to do to people's drinks and all that, so their destinies and decisions are what the world needs to continue existing."

"Yes," Jake replied. "But it doesn't work the same for everyone. Jay... I can barely make sense of the tangles. It's like someone used your hair as a path for the man's destiny. There's so much snarled up around him, you'd damn near think the entire world depended on that man's decisions and destiny. I'll need time to make sense of it. But the other one..."

"Tiran."

"Yes, Tiran. There's something about him. I couldn't tell, in part because of all the people in here. Plus, he was near you and Jay so much, but I swear, Aisling, it's like I'd look and look at him, and couldn't see a damn thing. Just the man. And a big dark void where the rest was supposed to be."

"What does that mean?"

"I don't know yet. There are rumors—things in lore, incidents I need to consult. And I may need to talk to The Management too."

"Will they deign to help you?"

"If it suits the world." Jake shook his head. "Sometimes, Aisling, I wish you could meet them. They deserve more credit than you might think."

"Well, I'm sure they're too busy running the world to take a meeting with a mere hostel proprietress."

"You know they stay parallel of you. You're off-limits, as far as Jakes and Jades go."

"I'll stick to the stout, all the same," Aisling replied.

"Don't you trust me?"

"Of course I trust you, older brother," Aisling

replied. "Just as much as Grandmother did. And like her, I also happen to consider GPS my favorite drink." Aisling stood up and drained her pint. "Now if you'll excuse me, I have a hostel to run… and a date to get ready for."

She didn't need to see his face. Connemara's scowl all but burned into her back as she left the pub. *Maybe I shouldn't wind him up like that*, Aisling thought. *He's doing his job and I've never had reason to distrust him. But The Management, the whole Jakes and Jades thing—it just creeps me out sometimes.*

She wandered through the city square, cutting south toward the hostel, which lay on a flat patch of scrubby grassland, just outside the cluster of buildings in the city center. To the east, the sun glowed on the hills.

Somehow, the mountain seemed to stay in shadow.

"You sure you don't want anything?" Jake asked. "At least some dinner. You look like you haven't eaten yet."

"No, Connemara."

"Aisling…"

"He said he'd meet me here." Aisling shrugged. "He's new in town. He's a traveler. Maybe he got lost."

"Lost? There are postage stamps bigger than

Clifden."

"Go pour a pint."

Alone again, Aisling sipped her water and stared at the pub entrance.

And stared.

By nine o'clock, still no Tiran.

She didn't look at Jake as she left. *Probably smirking,* she thought. *Maybe Tiran just forgot.*

Yeah, right.

When she left the dark night and closed the hostel door behind her, Aisling stood up straight and wide-eyed. The fire roared in the front room, but she could barely smell the peat.

Was that... garlic? And tomatoes with herbs? The air was all but golden with the scent, and she let it guide her to the hostel's small kitchen.

Just inside the doorway and to her right, Jay stood in front of the four-burner stove. Minced garlic and diced tomatoes sizzled in oil. Next to the pan, water simmered in a pot. The blue-gold flame of the gas burner flickered. Jay's green-gold eyes stared straight into her, and she wondered if he knew about Tiran, or about how she'd been stood up.

Jay just nodded at the pan and said, "What do you think?"

Aisling's stomach growled, and they both laughed. "I agree," Jay said. "More oregano." He picked up a small spice jar from the common shelf and shook light green leaves into the pan. "You hadn't eaten yet either, huh?" Jay said. "I always make extra. Care to join me?"

"Okay," Aisling said. "Can I help with anything?"

"There's a baguette you could slice and some GPS in the fridge if you fancy a beer."

Aisling looked from the pan to Jay's T-shirt and laughed again. "Really?" she said.

"I know. I know." Jay stared down at the words: "I Got Dried Out And Picked Up At The Salt And Crane, Clifden, Connemara, Ireland." He shrugged. "It's touristy as hell," he said, "but you gotta admit it's catchy."

As the beers settled in their glasses, Aisling sliced the baguette and then reached for the butter knife.

"Wait," Jay said, gently taking the knife from her fingers.

"It's bread, Jay. In Ireland, bread requires butter."

"When bread goes with spaghetti," Jay replied, "it requires garlic." He reached over to the cutting board, picked up a halved clove, and held it under Aisling's nose. "Take a deep breath."

"Of garlic?"

"Beautiful, unique, and um, aromatic. It's called the stinking rose, you know," Jay said. "Accurate, though not exactly flattering."

Aisling breathed in. It had never occurred to her before, all the aromas and their components, all the complexity behind the first punch of pungency. "Oh," she said. "It's rich and peppery and—"

"Exactly." Jay rubbed the bread slices all over with the cut garlic. "Now they're ready for butter," he said. "But with just that hint of garlic, it'll be perfect with the pasta."

Jay went back to the stove, adding an open can of tomato sauce to the pan.

"Where did you learn to cook?" Aisling asked, handing him a glass of stout.

"My mom," Jay replied. "I grew up in Idaho and my mom loved to cook. She was making pasta before pasta went west. You would've thought she'd been an Italian grandmother all her life."

"She and your dad must miss you."

"Yeah." Jay's shoulders stiffened. "I miss them too." He raised his glass. "Here's to those who miss us. May we always be home in their hearts, even if we're home on the road."

"That could be an Irish blessing," Aisling said.

"Maybe I should make a T-shirt out of it," Jay replied. They grinned at each other, clinked glasses, and drank deeply.

Aisling nodded at the pan. "So doesn't this need to simmer for hours or something?"

"Only if you want heartburn," Jay replied, dumping pasta into the pot of boiling water. "Long cooking like that makes a tomato sauce acidic as hell. The sauce will be ready when the pasta's done."

"Lucky for me I came when I did." *Don't mention Tiran,* she thought. *He doesn't want to either. Don't you dare go there.*

"I'd been out all afternoon looking around town," said Jay. "Figured I'd better make some dinner and unwind. Didn't expect anyone to come around."

"You didn't sniff the front room. I'm surprised half the hostel isn't here."

Jay laughed. "You're very kind."

"You said you always make extra. Why?"

Jay took a swig of his beer. "I had just arrived in Kenya, late as hell, and I was dragging. Roadblocks, a storm, and three breakdowns had turned the twelve-hour Nairobi bus ride to twenty hours. I'd run out of food and water, and was just down, down, down." He stirred the sauce and nodded. "It was nearly midnight when we got to Nairobi. I was so tired I could barely carry my pack, but I trudged on and found my way to a small hostel. There was no one at the desk; I just wrote a note on the counter, left some money, and dumped my bag at the nearest empty dorm bed."

"You must have been ready to just fall over."

"I was about to. Wouldn't have been the first time I'd gone to sleep hungry, and I figured I'd get up early as I could and find some food. But I'd hardly come out of the toilet when I smelled the most amazing scents coming from the kitchen. Rice. Peanuts. Chiles. I went downstairs and a man was cooking over a small hotplate. Tall. Skin like midnight. He looked me in the eye and then the biggest grin I'd ever seen came over his face."

They drained and plated the pasta, then added sauce and bread. As they sat at the small table in the back corner of the kitchen, Jay continued. "The man nodded and said, 'Bus?' I nodded back. 'I always make extra,' he said. 'You never know who will turn up.' He shared his meal with me. I ran back to my room—I always carry an, uh, emergency bottle of scotch—and we spent half the night talking. He was in Nairobi on business and to visit family. The next day he invited me to join him. We went all over the city, and I saw things and met people I never would have encountered had that bus arrived on time. After we went our separate ways, I resolved that anytime I cooked, I'd make extra." Jay tilted his glass to Aisling and smiled. "You never know who's going to turn up."

It's so easy to be around him, she thought, feeling her own grin widen. *So relaxing.* "Sounds like you've done a lot of traveling," Aisling said between bites. "This is amazing, by the way."

"Thank you," Jay replied. "I've traveled here and there, but I'm just one backpacker in a big world."

"Three years is a long time for any traveler."

A hollow look came into Jay's eyes. "I guess it is, now that you mention it. Funny thing is, when I started I figured I'd never stop." He shook his head.

"But I've nattered on enough about me. How did you wind up running a hostel?"

"I did a fair bit of traveling too," Aisling said. "I was sixteen when I left Clifden."

"Something tells me you didn't leave with your parents' blessing."

"No," Aisling said. "I hated it here. Thought Clifden was just a small forgotten spot of nothing in a larger forgotten spot of nothing. I had decided the world was for me, so I went to see it. And I did. London, Paris, New York, Portland, Santiago, Johannesburg, Sydney, Hong Kong. I made my way, kept my wits, and did okay."

"For how long?"

"Nine years."

"I must seem like a holidaymaker to you," Jay replied.

Aisling shrugged. "It wasn't always easy. Or fun. I say I kept my wits. Sometimes there was plenty going on that was trying to take them from me. But that's another story for another time. Main thing is, a little over three years ago..." The images flashed back into her mind: the eye, the river, the lightning. The afterimages faded from her memory, but for a moment it still seemed hard to see Jay. "The world was great, but well... I... I realized that I needed to come home. Clifden wasn't so bad after all, it seemed. There was a place for me here, and it turned out that the person running the hostel wanted to retire. He trained me up. I'd saved some money while working on the road, I bought the business from him, and, well, here I am."

"You're extraordinary."

"You're too kind."

"No, I mean it." Jay set down his glass and looked deep into her eyes. "You had to see the world. You had something you needed to run from. But in time, you came to understand that what mattered more was knowing what you wanted and loving it for what it was, for where you needed to be. That's admirable. Not everyone figures that out."

"Have you?"

Jay swallowed the last bite of his food. "Maybe I'm starting to."

They cleared away the dishes, and Aisling insisted on washing up. "I'm glad you turned up in Clifden," Aisling said, as hot water poured into the sink.

"You just like me for my pasta."

She laughed. "It does redeem your taste in T-shirts."

They stared at each other for a long moment.

"Look," he said, "I'm not very good at this. But if you're free sometime, would you, say, care to go for a walk with me? I'd love to see the hills around here, and it seems you know the place well."

A warm rush bloomed in her belly and spread all over her body. "I'd love to," Aisling replied before she could stop herself. "In fact, tomorrow morning I've got time. Game for an early rise?"

"I am if you are."

They stood silently, looking into each other's eyes. *He's kind,* Aisling thought. *Well traveled. He makes me laugh.*

And he is here.

A loud clinking noise made them both look at the sink.

"Ah, yes. The cleanup," Aisling said, trying to take a deep breath.

"I could keep you company, if you'd like."

"That's okay. You go on. I need to think about a few things anyway. Business stuff."

"Night then, Aisling."

"Night to you too, Jay."

Alone in the kitchen, Aisling started washing and rinsing the dishes. The day-to-day chores of the hostel had become meditative for her, a way to distance her mind from the world, letting the task at hand be both conduit and barrier. As the youngest Awen of Ireland in centuries, and the first with no prior Awen to directly guide or mentor her, Aisling had used these times to find her way. *Some would call me a seer,* Aisling thought. *Some—especially the Californians—seem partial to that word "shaman."*

She thought back to Jake Connemara standing before her, and regretted that it hadn't been her grandmother. Then she pulled herself back to the present and recited the oath that had sealed her role and fate:

"The world was the world and I was I. From now on, the world is I, and I am the world. I inspire, I guide, I protect. None will see my hand in events or know my mind. I unite the four, guard the three, and speak for the one. As long as the world dreams and breathes, I am its voice. From now until my death, I swear to be the Awen of Ireland and the world."

Awen. Connemara had told her that technically the word was Welsh and the Irish equivalent would have been "ai." Not even Grandmother had known how the title had been decided on. Connemara thought it an accident. Grandmother thought someone just figured "Awen" sounded better.

No matter the word, Aisling saw the effect. Sometimes people came to the hostel, devoid of excitement, empty of a love of life. After having a conversation and a cuppa tea with her—and there was always conversation and tea, or something stronger in particularly difficult cases—people moved on from Clifden ready to take on the world. Some stayed in touch, not that it mattered. One way or another, Aisling always knew what came of those who drank inspiration from the Awen of Ireland.

She set more clean dishes on a towel spread out on the counter. Not that she was grandiose. No one ever knew what she did, but from behind the scenes she had settled many a conflict in Clifden. A dispute between innkeepers, or an argument about land boundaries. A cheating husband or a vengeful wife. When Clifden flared, Aisling was there. Compromises were made, disputes were settled, new ways were found. Blood stayed in people's veins, but they remembered to let their hearts out, and that did everyone good. While no one ever seemed to realize what they were doing, they also come to her for wisdom, for advice. Connemara had said that's how it had been with her grandmother too; people just turned up, as if something in the land and in their blood showed them the way.

"Isn't it a lot of work just to keep a few people in a small town civilized?" she remembered asking Connemara.

"Not really," he'd replied. "Not when you understand what you're really doing."

"What am I really doing?"

"If I have to tell you," he said, "you won't know. When you know, you'll tell me."

"Are you being difficult?"

"That's what your grandmother told me to tell you when you asked."

Aisling finished the dishes and left the kitchen for her room. *I still don't fully understand,* she thought, as Jay's and Tiran's faces flashed in her mind like lightning.

Maybe that's where I'm going wrong.

* * * * *

THE WAITING HILLS looked west to the summit, where the traveler looked back at them.

"Why do they call them the Twelve Bens," Jay asked, "when I count thirteen?"

"Probably something to do with you Americans not being on the metric system," Aisling replied, standing next to Jay. *What the hell?* she thought. *How can he possibly see the mountain? No one has but me and Connemara.* "Don't be daft, Jay," she said. "We Irish can count, you know."

"I figured some Celtic myth must be behind it," Jay said. "Aye, sure. We call them the Twelve Bens, but really there's thirteen, and here's how that all came about." Jay waited, but Aisling just stared at him, one eyebrow raised. "No?" he said. "Really? Come on, there's got to be something. A fairy treasure mound. Where Blarney hid his moonshine from the English. The secret pens that survive from the old story about the cattle raid of Cooley." Jay paused again. "Nothing? Ah well. The thirteenth doesn't even look like the others. Seems more like a mountain than a hill."

"Maybe you can see Mount Everest from here."

Jay grinned. "So you really aren't kidding about the view."

"You can see nearly the whole world from the top of this hill, Jay," said Aisling. "But there are only twelve mountains. The Twelve Bens. Na Beanna

Beola. The name really is self-explanatory. Must be a trick of the fog. And here you are in that T-shirt. Is that what you Americans think of as irony?"

Jay glanced down. Beneath a pair of eyeglasses with Irish pint silhouettes for lenses, the shirt proudly told the world, "I Can See Clearly Now." Aisling watched him count the hills again. The fog shifted and the mountain seemed to wink.

A light breeze huffed up the hill. Instead of trying to lift Aisling's heavy red curls, the wind changed direction. Another breeze blew in, excited and puffing after its travels from a far corner of the world.

Jay took a deep breath of the misty early-morning air. "Weird," he said. "Do you smell something... hot?"

"No," Aisling replied. "I smell peat and mist. Pretty typical Irish morning."

"You don't smell, say, sunbaked cow flops or spices roasting in a dry pan?" Around them, green-brown hills rolled in the east. The blue-gray ocean lapped at Ireland's west, and in every other direction the world flowed.

"Um, no," Aisling replied. "We don't even have sheep up this way, much less sheep pellets." She kept her voice even, but her thoughts screamed at the mountain. *What is he doing here? What are you doing here? What are you doing to him?*

"You win," Jay said. "I wouldn't want to be

argumentative. Might get myself chucked out of the best hostel in Ireland."

"Eighth Wonder of the World, mate," she said.

"It's a good name," Jay replied. He sat on the scrubby moss and peat, then pulled a thermos of tea and two mugs out of his daypack. "Besides, the company's far better than the landscape, and what's the good of hills that can't count?"

Cut off by the tea steaming under her nose, Aisling sniffed a laugh and took the cup.

"Thanks for showing me the hilltop," Jay said.

"Least I can do after that dinner," Aisling replied. "Besides, I usually take this morning for a quiet walk to get the blood going." She chuckled. "That way I have at least one day where I don't start by cleaning vomit out of the sinks and flowerpots. Bloody English party blokes. Don't hold a glass if you can't hold your stout."

"Is that who did that?" Jay shook his head. "Damn, that was really rank. I'm just glad it wasn't me. We certainly wouldn't be here right now." Jay clinked his metal cup to hers. "Then I'd never know that in Ireland, thirteen hills can be considered twelve." He swayed toward Aisling and lightly bumped her shoulder.

Aisling smiled and sipped her tea. The light on the mountain made it seem like the hulking rock had given her a thumbs-up. For a moment, she sat still as the hills. Then she swallowed hard. "I suppose there must be trade-offs," she said.

"What do you mean?"

"You can say my name, but you make tea about as well as you count."

"I suppose we Yanks have our limitations."

They smiled at each other. The green-gold glint of Jay's eyes bounced off Aisling's blue. The breeze shifted and they turned away from the wind. "You traveled the world," Jay said, "but I see why you came back to Clifden and called it home."

"What makes you say that?"

Jay sipped and grimaced. "Tea," he said, shaking his head. "It's just not coffee. No. Thing is, I haven't been here long, but I've felt something I haven't felt in years. From the moment I got here, it's been there. Took me a while to figure it out."

"What is it?"

"I feel like I've come home."

Aisling started to say something but closed her mouth. She looked away from Jay, just to the side, but in her gazing she had put on a pack, grabbed a passport, and was already halfway around the world. Desert sun washed out the hills. For a moment, Jay stood in a shadow of angled lines that stopped at a sharp point. Then the green, wet hills of Ireland came back into sight, unreal in the foggy morning sky.

The mountain looked angry.

"Yesterday I had an Irish breakfast for a late

lunch," Jay said. "I could get used to that."

Aisling chuckled. "Until the heart attack."

"It'd keep the day from going boring, I suppose—and the town, and the countryside right around. Your here and now has so much *then*. Every step I take, I feel like I'm walking on centuries. I hear the language and my blood seems to catch fire. I want to run and shout and dash from one end of the country to another."

Aisling tried to grin but some anger kept stirring in her, as if the mountain and the world were trying to tell her something was wrong.

Jay looked away. "Sorry," he said. "I get a little carried away sometimes. After so long on the road, on my own, things get grinding. I traveled... for my own reasons... but when I went to The Blast Memorial yesterday, something changed."

"It has a big effect on people," Aisling replied. "I don't think I ever loved or appreciated life as much as I have since I first saw it."

"All that desolation. All those people who died—I mean, not just in what was Galway, but all over the world. The fires..." A shudder rippled through Jay. "It's like, I know they're called the Black Cliffs of Dover. I've seen pictures, and read that they were white until The Blast scorched them black as it burned England. It's one thing to know that, but to see it... They were so much darker than I ever knew, like a wound, a hole in the world. But even after seeing that, I still can't imagine how terrifying The Blast must have been. I just wonder if more people died from fear than from fire."

"Aye," Aisling said, "but people say it changed the world. "War has all but ended. Slavery is no more. Nations suppressed by colonial powers regained their sovereignty—all the more so, given how many of the rebuilding funds and materials for Britain and Ireland came from nations in Africa and Asia."

"Seeing The Blast Memorial brought home to me how precious and fragile life is," Jay said. "How much it's affected everything that's happened since, like you said. And it made me take a look at myself. I've traveled for so long. After getting here yesterday and feeling that sense of home bloom inside me, it's like I don't have a reason to travel anymore."

The anger of the world and the mountain now poured into Aisling. "What are you getting at?" she asked, trying to keep her voice even. *I am the Awen of Ireland,* she thought, *and rage will do no good here... I don't know why it's so important to a hunk of rock that Jay get back on the road, but I'm hardly going to throw him on a bus to Dublin...*

"When I heard you playing those tunes, it hit me. This country here, the people. This... this is Ireland. Right down to Irish eyes like yours, Aisling. A country that's known a lot of living. Fierce and true and beautiful." He looked away, to the ocean and to the hills, and to the world flowing in all directions. He turned back and stared her in the eyes. "I don't want to travel anymore," he said. "After three years, I've done what I needed to do. I've gone where I needed to go. There's so much else to see, of course, but you can't go everywhere. There's so much world and so few years. My travels have been amazing, from each ten-hour bus ride to all of the nights I pretty much slept on the toilet, but I'm done." Jay shook his head. "I want nothing more than to stay in Clifden." He smiled. "I want to settle down."

"Done traveling?" Aisling shook her head. "You sounded like a lifer. You're the kind of bloke one would think would never stop traveling. The world is your home sort of thing."

Jay shrugged. "I thought that too. I thought... I thought it was something I had to do. But I've done enough now." He stood up. "I'm staying, Aisling. A flat, a job, my own pint glass down the pub. I want it all. I want to live here. Hang up my backpack. I know I'm not from here, but I... I could be of here."

Aisling stood up and looked long at the traveler. Then she turned and stared to the east. In the distance, fog crumbled away from the hills. Her smile faded. "I understand where you're coming from." She looked back at Jay. "Well then, let's see what Clifden has for a globetrotting American who wants to better himself."

"What do you mean?"

"You want to become Irish," she said. "That's an upgrade if ever I've heard of one." *Besides*, she thought, *I've got to get away from this mountain. The glare's damn near burning me, and I can't figure this out yet.*

They packed up and walked down the hill. At the road toward Clifden and the hostel, Aisling stumbled. She got her footing back just before tumbling to the ground, yet she could see no rock or tangle of scrub in her way. *It's like the path shifted,* she thought, *and caught my feet in the process.*

Ahead, a thin strip of white stood stark against the brown of the peat bogs and the gray-black asphalt of the road.

Aisling stopped walking and looked all around. "The conversation distracted me," she said. "We should be back by now. This is the road out of town, not the road back to the hostel. We're at the edge of town. Beyond that sign is just the rest of the world."

Jay walked up to the sign. Down the post from the top, brown-black letters spelled "CLIFDEN." Time and weather had cracked and dulled the post's white paint, but light seemed to intensify as it reflected off the surface. Nailed all over the post, the arrowed ends of white boards showed the way to the parts of the world they pointed to:

New York, USA. 4,881 km/3,033 miles
Cairo, Egypt. 4,214 km/2,618 miles
Dublin, Ireland. 251 km/156 miles
Agamuskara, India. 8,225 km/5,111 miles
Tierra del Fuego, Argentina. 13,136 km/8,163 miles
Sydney, Australia. 17,375 km/10,796 miles
Bangkok, Thailand. 10,094 km/6,272 miles
Tír na nÓg: 0

"Tier-nuh-nog?" Jay asked.

"It's said to be the Land of the Young," Aisling replied. "The land of everlasting youth and life. A sort of heaven. Stories say it's an island far to the west of Ireland."

"So why does the sign say we're right on it?"

"Some might say this used to be it. But the wise would say that heaven is right where you are standing."

"Interesting touch."

"I helped put up the sign when I was a girl," Aisling said. "My grandmother brought in this man, and they did most of the work. He was dressed all in black, and there was something about his face. It's like he could have been from anywhere." Her mind went back all those years. "He and Grandmother said the sign would be a nice way to remind everyone how much world there is and how, of course, Ireland is at the center of it all." She didn't mention the rest—how when they were done, the man had touched her shoulders and locked the gaze of his brown-black eyes on hers. "You will be magnificent," he said. "And one day, you will see me again."

"The Celtic Meridian?" Jay asked, pulling her back to the present.

"Precisely," Aisling said. "That's actually what we call it." She frowned. "Funny, though. I don't remember some of these. Agamuskara, India?" She glanced at Jay, then back to the sign. "Never heard of it."

If he had heard her voice shake, he didn't show it.

At the time, Aisling thought, *I figured it would be a simple sign that showed Clifden's distance to other major cities, though I never understood then why anyone would ever think of Clifden as a major city. There was nothing important about Clifden, I believed at the time. Grandmother had just smiled at me when I told her this. Said that perhaps someday I'd see my home differently.*

"Maybe someone's added more," Jay said.

Only after becoming Awen had Aisling learned the secret of the white sign; the cities it showed changed, depending on the destinies of those who were looking at the sign.

Except for me, Aisling thought. *It never pointed me toward some different place—some Anywhere Else, Somewhere Else, or Everywhere Else. I stood before it when*

I turned sixteen, begging it to show me where to go, but the post was empty. It only showed me Clifden. So I left. Of course, it was Agamuskara, Bangkok and Cairo that brought me back...

"Aisling?" Jay asked. "Are you okay?"

She shrugged and turned her back on the sign. "Let's go, Jay," she said. "This time I promise you, we'll be at the hostel in no time, and there'll be a proper cuppa tea to warm us."

"Let me ask you something," Jay said.

"Okay."

"Here's the thing. So Tír na nÓg is right where I am standing. We just wound up seeing that sign, then that sign must be a sign that I'm where I belong. Since I have come home, I should stay."

Aisling said nothing.

Jay sighed. "So you aren't going to answer that?"

"You weren't really asking a question," she said. "But I will tell you this. You don't know the point of what you're doing anymore. I've felt that way after tourist season."

"What do you do?"

Aisling smirked. "Lock the door."

Jay laughed.

"No, really. I lock the door, sip whiskey by the fire, and tell the world to feck off awhile."

"How long does that last?"

"Till the next morning. Then I can manage again." Aisling touched his hand. "Funny thing about the world, Jay. There's truly no rest for the wicked, the wondrous, and the wandering. Sometimes it seems that all life does is push you forward, regardless of how you feel about it. Then it gives you the breather you need so you can pick up and go onwards again."

"Are you saying I need a breather?"

"I'm saying let's see how you get. Spend some time getting to know Clifden better. Stuff your arteries with more Irish breakfasts. Lighten the pub of its excess stout. Then you can figure out your place in the world and whether or not this is it."

They walked the rest of the way to the hostel in silence. The fog faded. Around them, the Irish day stretched, rolled out of bed, and put the kettle on.

"Nearly home," Aisling said, smiling. "You'll soon see the hostel gleaming, just beyond that hill."

They stopped for a moment. The touch of Jay's skin still lingered on her hand. The mountain still screamed, but Aisling just stared at his face, seeing only the kiss that could be, the kiss that should be.

Jay's eyes narrowed. "Smoke," he said.

"What?"

Jay started to run. "There's smoke rising."

Aisling ran too, soon catching up to Jay. They came around the small hill, and thicker, blacker smoke rolled into the sky.

They ran faster toward the fire pouring from the small white hostel.

* * * * *

THE FIREMAN blocked her way again. "In case you missed it," he said, "there's been a fire."

"It's my feckin hostel," Aisling replied. "I need to get in there."

"Yours or not, you're not getting near it yet," the fireman said. "It's too hot."

He turned away from Aisling, and she kicked the ground.

"At least the damage is minor," Jay said. "It could have been so much worse. Looks like most of the place is fine. It's just the kitchen that got hit pretty hard."

"And one of the dorms," came a voice. "Ours, I believe."

Tiran walked up from behind them. "I came as soon as I heard," he said, reaching for Aisling's hand. "Are you okay?"

"So that's what it takes to make a fella show up," she replied, pulling her hand away. "I've things to tend to, lads. I'll let you know when you can see if your things survived."

Aisling felt their eyes on her as she walked away. Jay no doubt would have noticed how he suddenly was at arm's length. If Tiran didn't realize she was mad at him, then he was too stupid to hold a beer and listen to the fiddle at the same time. She stared at the smoking blackened lumber that used to be the kitchen. Jay did have a point. The entire hostel could have been lost. People could have been hurt or killed. As luck had it, everyone had already left the hostel for their day's adventures when the fire started.

The fireman was now talking with a police officer, so Aisling beelined to them. "Aisling," they both said, with a quick nod.

"Do you know anything yet?"

The officer shrugged. "Far as we can tell, the plug-in kettle had gone faulty. So had the gas line supplying the cooker. Eventually, the kettle sparked and enough gas had built up to start a small explosion and then the fire."

"So it was an accident."

"Of course, Aisling," said the fireman. "You don't exactly get many arsonists in Clifden. Too wet to bother, really. They'd lose patience and go where the flames don't drip."

"This is my place, Finn."

Even under the soot on his cheeks, Aisling could see the fireman blush. "No disrespect meant, Aisling."

"Just let me in there. I need to know. I need to see for myself."

"It's hot."

Color rose in her face. "It'll be your son's birthday candles compared to what I'm about to be."

The two men stared at each other. *It's amazing the conversations men can have without saying a single bloody word*, Aisling thought.

Finally, they both sighed and nodded. "Okay, Aisling," the officer said. "You can go in. But for heaven's sake, be careful."

"At least take these," said the fireman. "They're not totally fireproof, but you can move things."

Aisling nodded and accepted the thick gloves. "Thank you."

"Give a shout if you need us."

The mist had come back and was helping to further cool the heat and knock down the smoke. Still, she heard the clinks and pops of the blackened coals that had been the kitchen. She tried to match the desolation before her to the warm, lively room she had known so well. She stared at the corner where she and Jay had sat the night before.

She shook her head. *I'm not here to reminisce.*

The floor had been large white tiles, perfectly spaced and angled. All had shattered in the heat, their white glazes black with fire and soot, their perfect squares now jumbled all around.

Except one.

Aisling walked to the middle of the room. *The previous owner never did know,* she thought. *Everyone agreed he was safer that way. If I weren't the Awen, I wouldn't know either. I'd walk over it every day and never be the wiser to what was under my own floor.*

Turning to check every angle, Aisling made sure no one could see her. Satisfied, she put on the thick fire gloves and kneeled down in what had been the middle of the kitchen. She brushed away rubble until a perfect white square showed.

To be honest, she thought, *if you know where to look it's not exactly hard to get what you're looking for.*

She'd often wondered if the setup created more trouble than it was worth. Then again, it had been decades since anyone had tried to take the relics. Was this really an accident? Had a thief used the fire as cover? And if it was, would she find nothing inside but ash, or broken pieces, or—

With a deep breath, Aisling pulled the tile free and looked into the space beneath. *Maybe it's still there,* she thought. *Maybe he was trying to destroy it, though no fire could burn that wooden goblet. Or maybe he wasn't able to find it.*

When she saw, she knew. She'd known from the moment she'd seen the smoke. For a moment, Aisling closed her eyes. The goblet was gone. *The first of the three has been stolen,* she thought. *It's begun.*

She put the tile back in place and covered the white with soot and rubble.

"I will get it back," she said. "I have to get it back."

The world is now at stake, she thought, *but that is too much to consider. One thing at a time, Aisling. Deal with what's in front of you.* She stood and walked toward the burned dorm. *Small miracles,* she thought. *Everyone's beds, backpacks, and* possessions hadn't been burned, except...

Jay's bed had burned, though his pack was unscathed. Aisling shook her head. *Can't imagine how the pack didn't get so much as singed,* she thought. *Feck, you'd think it had walked away and come back or something.*

Jay, she thought. *Tiran. It has to be one of them. Where did Tiran disappear to last night? And Jay... he knows his way around a kitchen. He'd know how to cover his tracks.*

Is it one of them? Is it both of them?

And right now, they know I'm angry with them...

She closed her eyes and breathed in the misty air. *I'm the Awen of Ireland,* she thought, willing her anger to dissolve into the mist. *My test is here. My time is now. Anger will not save the other two relics.*

She opened her eyes and walked to where she could see Jay and Tiran again. The two men stood where she had left them, and they seemed to be chatting. *I have to keep them close,* she thought. *Both of them. They're going to help me. While they're thinking I don't know what's going on, one of them will reveal to me what he really knows and who he really is.*

One of them will tell me he's the thief.

I will see this through, Aisling thought. *Before the other relics are stolen. Before the threat can become real.*

She stared at the smoking ruins.

Before someone gets hurt.

* * * * *

HAMMERING RANG across the lowland. Aisling walked faster, wanting to find out what the noise was. Her mind raced back along the frantic day.

She'd talked with the fire department. The police now had a statement. After some cheerily fiery haggling, a local contractor had given her a reasonable estimate to clean up and rebuild. The police had judged the rest of the hostel to be safe, and they had allowed it to reopen, as long as Aisling boarded off the burned areas. That still needed to be done.

Jay, Tiran, and the other people in that dorm had to be turned out, but Aisling had refunded the rest of their stay and directed them toward inns and spare rooms in town.

Everyone should be sorted by now, she thought doubtfully. Word was, six large Deep Travel buses of tourists had just come in from New Galway, and most of the rooms would be spoken for already.

Grandmother never dealt with anything like this, Aisling thought. *Megalomaniacs, crazy presumptive world dominators, and tyrants—sure. Grandmother was shot at. Nearly blown up a few times. Plus, there was that bloke who tried to throw her off the Bens. Until I became Awen and Jake told me otherwise, I always thought the duel was just a scary story she'd made up.*

But no one had ever tried to burn down her house.

Back then, the logic had made so much sense.

After all, the second relic, the walking stick, was hidden in Connemara's pub. It had virtually around-the-clock protection and oversight from a Jake of the Jakes and Jades. The goblet was already hidden beneath the hostel, so why not have the Awen be there as its guardian?

Of course, the third relic had no such security. Aisling's mind drifted to the cave in the Twelve Bens, and she shuddered. *Then again,* she thought, *the box has its own protections.*

The hostel came into view. The crackle of flames had been replaced by the sounds of hammering and sawing. As Aisling came around the front to where the kitchen had been, the sound stopped.

Jay and Tiran lifted a sheet of plywood into place where the hallway wall and kitchen doorway had been. It was the last in a line of sheets they had fastened to that wall and the adjoining wall. As Jay held the sheet in place, Tiran nailed it to fresh lumber. When they were done, the men stepped back and examined their work. While their expressions held a satisfaction with what they'd done, a wary, tense argument seemed to pass wordlessly between them.

"We heard this needed to be closed off from the rest so you could reopen," Tiran said. "Figured we'd take care of it."

"How did you get the plywood here?" Aisling replied. "Surely, you didn't carry it."

"A taxi will carry anything," Jay said with a grin. "As long as the fare's right."

Aisling looked at the panels and smiled. "Well, thank you," she said. "That's quite a help."

"It was Tiran's idea."

You both confuse me, Aisling thought. *Jay makes me feel too at ease. Tiran blew me off last night, but even now, whenever I look at him... What is your game, you two?* "Maybe I needn't have bothered talking to the lads in town," Aisling said. "If you're staying on a bit, you'll have the kitchen rebuilt by teatime."

"I have to admit," Tiran said, "I wasn't planning to be in Clifden more than a couple of days." He smiled at Aisling. "But with what I've found here, I have to stay on a bit longer."

"Yeah, me too," Jay said. "You know how it goes. You have to figure out the good that can come from the bad things that have already happened. I'm taking the fire as a sign that what I told you earlier was right: Clifden is telling me that the hostel isn't for me. I shouldn't be in a hotel or inn or something, which, you know, is good, since all the rooms are suddenly full up. I should find a flat, a place of my own. I'm going to stay, Aisling. I told you I felt at home here. Even with all that's happened today, with what I've found here, I feel more at home than ever."

Out of sight behind the men, the Twelve Bens stood faint in the mist. But the mountain flared out, as if covered in bright summer sun at noon, but with the redness of a fierce sunset.

Why are you angry? Aisling thought. *What do you care if some backpacker wants to move to Clifden? You can't fault his taste, after all.*

The mountain waited and then Aisling understood.

But you can fault his motives...

She stared hard at Jay. *Damn you,* she thought. *It has to be you who started the fire. Genius, too. You were in the kitchen for ages—more than enough time to find the panel and steal the goblet, then sabotage the kettle and gas line. And what do we do? We go for a walk. Perfect alibi: you weren't there at the time. Couldn't have been you. Oh no. With your good pasta and your beautiful eyes and how easily you make me laugh and want to—*

"Are you okay?" Jay asked. "Aisling?"

Jay wants to stay because he wants to find the other relics, she thought. *He wants to stay because he's puzzled it out. And once he has the relics, who would want to leave? The source of their power is here, and those who crave power always stay close to its source.*

Damn you, she thought. *Damn you.* Color rose in her cheeks, and as her anger welled the damp air crackled.

But while Aisling raged inside, the Awen smiled back at the men. *Not yet,* she thought. *Not yet. Awen.* "I'm okay," she replied. "It's just been a hard day, as you can imagine."

The words whispered through her mind: "Stay close to those who seek to stay close to power." The voice had been Connemara's, but the words were Grandmother's.

Aisling's inner anger turned to outward sweetness. "Jay, it's a fine idea for you to stay." *If my words had color, they'd be a sickly green.* "Here, I'll give you some names of folks who may have rooms to let. That'll help you find your feet." After Jay fished out a notebook and pen from his pack, Aisling wrote down names and addresses.

"Thank you," Jay said. "I'll start asking around as soon as we're done here."

"Actually, you've done enough for the day," Aisling said. "Helping me like this is such a kindness. Go sort yourself out. Maybe we can meet down the pub later."

Jay nodded and they gave good-byes. Aisling and Tiran stood next to each other as Jay wandered off, his pack on his back as he headed toward town.

He cannot stay, the mountain said. *Whatever you must do, whatever it takes, he must not stay.*

Whatever it takes, Aisling thought. *He will leave. I won't let him get the relics.* She waited for a reply, but the mountain said no more.

"He's a nice guy," said Tiran. "Though sometimes I think he can be a bit too nice. You know what I mean?"

Aisling glared at him. "I appreciate what you did

today. I do. But." Tiran locked his eyes on hers, and her mind blanked. A heat raced through Aisling, and it left no room for breath or thought.

"I'm sorry I stood you up," Tiran said. "You're right. I was an arse. And yes, I fixed up the plywood today to try to make amends."

Dammit, she thought, *looking at him is even worse than looking at Jay. Now start breathing again.* "So why weren't you there last night?"

"I lost someone once, someone beyond dear to me," Tiran replied. "When it happened, everything in my life changed. Who I am. Who I thought I was. It's like my entire world, my entire self, has been different ever since. Since then I've just wandered, trying to make a fresh start. It's been hard. More difficult than I ever could have imagined." He looked away. "I stood you up last night because every time I look at you I get this excited feeling. This hope, this anticipation... this contentment that I haven't felt since much happier days."

She stared hard at him. "Happiness is not easy to come by in this life, it's said."

"Nothing worthwhile is," Tiran replied.

We're standing really close, Aisling thought. *When did I start holding his hand?*

"I don't think I've ever had that sort of happiness," Aisling said, as they turned and faced each other. "But every time I look in your eyes, it's like the sun rises inside me."

"I've never known anyone like you," Tiran said.

"Would you like to?" Aisling replied.

She shut her eyes as his closed. Tiran's lips were as soft as Irish rain, as refreshing as a pint, as warm as an Egypt morning.

We're much too close now, she thought, but as the sun rose in her and warmed her, the woman and the Awen faded until all she felt was the kiss, the kiss, the kiss.

II

As Jay slid in to the chair across the table from Aisling, he looked like he was beginning to fray, which was good, but he still seemed much too relaxed for her satisfaction. "With the way the week's been," Jay said, "I've kept meaning to come to the restaurant part of the pub. Can't believe I'm only just now getting to have the Irish breakfast here."

"The Salt and Crane has the best in Ireland," Aisling replied. "Though I don't think there's yet a T-shirt to commemorate it. You'll have to settle for the food." Upstairs the pub slept, but around them in the street-level restaurant, tourists and locals laughed, or tucked in silently to their Irish breakfasts, as if in prayer or reverie. Aisling added milk to her tea, the spoon clinking as she stirred. "How you keeping?"

"It's been rough," Jay said. "I must have knocked on every door and checked at every front desk in town. No rooms. No beds. Seems like I can hardly walk into a place, what with all the tour groups around."

"You know, I'm sorry the hostel has been packed," she said.

"And Tiran got to that one open bed before I did." Jay nodded. "I know how it goes. First come, first serve."

"Where have you been sleeping?" *And what the hell is it going to take to get you out of here?*

"The park, the town square, a couple of alleys." Jay smiled. "I've had worse. At least it's a nicer time of year. The way the mist falls overnight, it's almost like a blanket."

He should've given up by now, Aisling thought. Grandmother said that when someone came for the relics, the Awen's job began with making Clifden inhospitable, in hopes of getting the would-be thief to give up the chase. *Jay's had no place to sleep,* Aisling thought. *He looks haggard as hell, but he's still got that cheeky grin and a light in his eyes. Does this mean that he has the goblet? One relic down, two to go, don't give up now?*

A server walked over. "Have you ordered yet?" Jay

asked. "Boy could I do with a coffee."

Aisling grinned. "I've been coming here since I was a little girl," she said, "and I've always gotten the same thing: a bowl of porridge." She smiled, but the Awen of Ireland focused.

"Coffee and a full Irish breakfast, please," Jay said to the server.

"Coming right up," she replied.

"Thank goodness," Jay said. "I've been on bread, jam, cheese, and stout all week. I could do with a hearty meal and a hot cuppa."

A few minutes later, the server set a mug of tea on the table. *No steam,* Aisling thought. *Well, I hadn't planned for it to be cold, but it's a nice touch.*

"Excuse me." Jay pointed to the mug. "I asked for a coffee."

The server shrugged. "Coffee just went eejit on us. Only tea now."

"But this is cold."

"Oh." She smiled. "Kettle died too. Sorry. I'll bring a hot one if I can get one."

She left and Jay stared at the mug. "Isn't cold tea in the morning a war crime?"

"We're not at war," Aisling replied. *Not exactly,* she thought. *I just want you gone. But there's no need to be hostile about it.*

Yet.

Jay poured milk and sugar into the tea. "If it can't be hot, at least it can be sweet," he said. "You know what's really weird, though?"

"What?" Aisling said, trying to keep her attention focused on the kitchen.

"Every time I think I've got my sense of direction figured out, I don't." Jay took a sip and grimaced. "The Thirteen Bens—"

"Twelve."

"I still count thirteen. Either way, they're still to the east. Should be easy, you know, with such a prominent, easily visible landmark. But every time I'm walking somewhere—around town, nipping to the hostel—I wind up on that same path we got lost on. Next thing I know, I'm in front of that sign. But that's not the weird part." He took another sip of tea and grimaced again. "The arrows are always different."

"Different?" *That's never happened*, Aisling thought. *They always stay the same for someone looking at them.*

"I end up there multiple times a day," Jay said, "including this morning. That's why I was late meeting you, in fact. This time there were only two arrows."

"What did they say?"

"One still showed Agamuskara, India." The gleam in Jay's eyes flickered. "Another sign pointed in the opposite direction. 'Idaho, USA,' it said. 'Seven thousand one hundred sixty-six kilometers or four thousand four hundred fifty-three miles.'"

One or the other, Aisling thought. *Go forward or go back. But I don't know why it's so stark for him. And the mountain still isn't talking...*

"I mean, Idaho, of all places," Jay said, nudging the mug away from him. "That's no place to travel. It was just a feckin place to have come from. It's like the sign was telling me to leave. Go on or go home." Anger rose in his voice. "But you know what? I'm not going back to where I came from. My new home is here. If I ever make my way to India, I'll be happy to do so in my dreams."

The server set a hot bowl of porridge in front of Aisling. "That's so minimal," Jay said, then beamed as the massive platter of his Irish breakfast was placed before him. Grease shimmered on two long sausages. The yin and yang of the white pudding and black pudding enticed with their mysterious contents. "I prefer my oats in sausage form," he said, breathing in the rich, spicy scents.

"And your blood too."

"I'm excited about the black pudding, actually. Blood as pudding. I can't see that getting hocked back in the States."

"A-fear-icans," Aisling said, staring at the food. "Yanks are always so squeamish about the wide world. Don't know what you were missing. Present company excepted, of course."

The browned bacon smiled at the two yellow and white fried eggs. "I understand the fried potatoes,"

Jay said, then pointed to the red islands in a choppy sea of baked beans. "But tomatoes?"

"Veggies," Aisling replied. "Gotta be healthy nowadays."

"I'm not going to be daunted, though," he said. "I'm not talking about breakfast. I'm talking about Clifden. I won't get discouraged. I won't stop trying. Turn me about all day. Walk the soles off my boots. I don't care. I've come home. I'm staying. I'm getting a giant breakfast and a flat. Nothing's going to stop me. Besides, at least the room part just got easier."

No, Aisling thought. *There's no way. Everyone knows not to let to Jay. A word here, a hint there; one way or another, they're put off, though no one of course is going to say so. They don't even know why. They just know not to. Around here, that's enough.*

"Yeah, I lucked out," Jay continued. "Jake Connemara, the bartender bloke, he stopped me on the way in. Said there was a spare room above the pub that I could use. I dropped off my stuff on the way in."

She'd been staring at the breakfast platter for so long, that for a moment Aisling saw only red and white. *Dammit Connemara,* she thought. *You know Jay can't stay here.*

A skin of dark grease quivered on the little black disc of hot blood, spices, and oats. Fork and knife in hand, Jay hovered for an appreciative moment over Ireland's proof that you can eat blood with a fork.

"At last," Jay said. The tines pierced.

The blood pudding unclotted and fell off the fork. A small puddle jiggled on the plate as Jay sat back.

Aisling swallowed a spoonful of porridge. "Perhaps that sheep was a hemophiliac," she said. *Did I just destroy Jay's breakfast?* she thought. *How the hell did I do that?*

"It... it melted," Jay said. Before he could try anything else on the plate, black spicy blood flooded the potatoes, the tomatoes, the beans, and the white pudding. At each touch, the beans unbeaned, the potatoes mashed themselves into goo, the tomatoes sauced, and the white pudding puddled. Something more akin to a toilet after a dodgy meal stared back at Jay.

Crack, she thought. *Just crack. Realize you did wrong. Realize it's not worth it. Leave. Please.*

Unmoving, Jay stared at what had been a perfect Irish breakfast. "How could this have happened?" he asked. "Food doesn't melt like that. But after everything else that's been going wrong, what the hell, why not?" A thin, high laugh started to stumble out of his mouth.

He set down his fork and knife, looked up at Aisling, and the grin came back. The light gleaming off his smile could outshine sausage grease. "This is one hell of a story!" He laughed, but the pitch and warble of his laughter was anything but easygoing.

People at other tables looked over at them. "The melting Irish breakfast," Jay said. "But you know what? Not every day on the road is new friends and free beer."

He closed his eyes and shook his head. When he looked at Aisling again, something wild and frantic gleamed back. "Some days the only thing I can be grateful for is that only a small bit of cash in my pocket got nicked. Some days I'm lucky to leave the toilet. Some places I've just taken my pack off the bus and wished the next bus left sooner than next week. Today's the worst. No, second worst, but that's another story for another time. But today is different from any bad day I've had traveling."

"How's that?"

His gaze softened, mellowed. "It's my last day traveling and my first day home. Today's the day. I know it. I feel it. You have to know when it's time to take your boots off."

Jay waved over the server and pointed at his plate. "I don't know what happened here," he said, "but I think it's fair to ask for another Irish breakfast."

"Fair enough's the asking," the server replied, "but the kitchen just closed for lunch." She walked away before Jay could say anything else.

Aisling set down her spoon. "Are you sure those signs are telling you to stay here? You want to call Clifden home. I get that." *Get out get out get out,* she thought, reaching over for Jay's hand. "Maybe Ireland doesn't share your feelings."

"Ireland doesn't know what it's missing."

"Maybe Ireland knows what it wants to miss."

"What do you mean? Ireland doesn't want me to stay?" Jay's voice was low and hard. "It's just a place. It doesn't have feelings."

"Then despite all that traveling, maybe you don't know much about places after all."

"I know what's right for me."

"No," Aisling said. "You know what you think is right for you. No matter how much we try otherwise, the world has a way of helping us find the path where our feet need to be."

Jay shook his head. "The world happens to people, yes, but people also happen to the world. The rest is response. The rest is choice. Often what we do, we do in spite of what goes on in the world, not because of it. Tell me, Aisling, do you want me to stay?"

No, she thought. *I want you to leave. Because the mountain wants you to leave. Because I can't stand that you came here to take the relics. Because you could be such a good—*

You must leave.

She stared hard at Jay. "What I want, or don't want, isn't what matters right now. You're meant to be a traveler. You're meant to be on the road, not off it." She smiled. "Tell me true, Jay of the road, can you really look deep inside and see yourself reading the paper on Sundays or pruning the roses in the spring or going to the same pub to see the same people and say the same things every night? Can you really see yourself doing that? Because I can't."

"You hardly know me." Jay stood.

"I know you well enough to know that you staying in one place is how you try to run from who you really are."

"No," Jay said. "You don't. I was once perfectly happy to be nowhere else but home. In the same town where I grew up, even. I'd never planned to leave. I'd never planned to go anywhere. Then... things happened. I had to leave. I'll never go back; that's true. And I've seen a lot of the world; that's true too. But I crave home again. I crave the sameness and comfort of being in one place and knowing there's a sliver of the world that I can call my own."

Aisling nodded. "I know that's what you think you want, but you're wrong."

"This is pointless," Jay replied. "You don't want me here, fine. You prefer Tiran, fine. But I prefer here. And one way or another, I'm staying." He glanced at the plate. "And I'm sure as hell not paying for that."

She watched the door shut behind him. Then she finished her porridge and drank her tea. As she left, she set enough money on the table for the whole tab.

"Connemara!" Aisling climbed the stairs to the pub. "I could bloody kill you right now!"

Before she could touch the door, it swung open.

Jake looked up from a newspaper and sipped his coffee. "What's wrong?" he asked.

"What's wrong?" Aisling answered. "What's bloody wrong? I just melted a plate of breakfast and somehow made Jay more determined than ever to stay here," she said, standing above him. "And how does that happen? When he's finally starting to bloody crack? Because it turns out Jake-the-feckin-eejit-bartender-Connemara gave him a feckin room!"

"Aisling. It's okay." Jake walked over to a small patch of wall between the end of the bar and a doorway that led to the small upstairs room where Jay would be staying. When he pressed a certain spot just so, a panel swung open. Jake reached inside and took out a slender walking stick, worn with time. One end was tipped in brass; the other end had been smoothed and shined from years of being held.

"It's not okay and you know he can't stay," she replied. "You know that whatever's going on, that bloody mountain out there is determined Jay should leave Clifden. You know Jay stole the goblet and set my hostel on fire. And in return, you practically hand him the second relic. One more and he has the set. You know the stakes. If the relics are combined..."

"The walking stick is right here," Jake said. "What's more, I don't think Jay is behind the goblet and the fire."

"Then you're bloody blind."

Jake returned the stick and closed the panel. "Says the person snogging the other bloke we should be keeping a close eye on."

"How do you know about that? And Tiran's quite the gentleman. It's only been a few snogs, thank you."

"A few too many. But since Jay and Tiran don't give me heart palpitations, red cheeks, and shortness of breath, I have to point out that Jay seems far less suspicious to me than Tiran."

"You're only saying that because he doesn't like your pub."

They now stood inches from each other. "Are you even listening to yourself right now, Aisling? You sound like a teenager," Jake said. "I thought I'd be talking with the Awen of Ireland about the biggest threat to the relics in decades."

"You are."

"Really? Then how about you try trusting me. Goodness knows your grandmother did."

"I'm not Grandmother."

"Neither of us expected you to be," Jake said, his face reddening and his eyes narrowing. "But we would've thought you'd keep your head when it mattered."

"Who the hell are you to criticize me?"

"I'm not saying Jay's without suspicion," said Jake. "I'm saying we can't rule Tiran out. He doesn't add up. He's hiding something. I wish I could get another look at him so I could read his potential destinies, but curiously enough I can never seem to get near the man."

"Jay is that damn-near-mythical traveler we keep hearing about," Aisling said. "You know that, right?"

"It makes sense to me. He fits everything we've heard. It's probably also why The Management told me I wasn't to influence him. What's happening with his destiny right now is something that we can't interfere with."

"I'm betting it's gone to his head. He's gotten grandiose notions. And who knows what we haven't been hearing. Have you thought about that? How in the hell can you let him stay here?"

"The Management only said I couldn't influence him." Jake grinned. "They didn't say anything about refusing hospitality to a man who's been sleeping in doorways for a week. I'm not a man to forget his manners."

"Didn't think you were a man at all."

"I'm trying to help you, Aisling," Jake said. "Please. See clearly."

"I am seeing clearly," Aisling replied. "And you

know what? I'm the bloody Awen of Ireland. Not you. You're always telling me what to do, always poking your nose in. I don't care that Grandmother confided in you. But I no longer need you to be my self-appointed mentor. Do your feckin job, Jake Connemara. But from now on, stay out of my way so I can do mine."

Before he could say anything else, Aisling turned and went down the stairs, out into a misty morning that felt colder than it had when she'd first gone inside.

Off to the east, the mountain glowered.

"Oh, shut up," Aisling said.

EIGHT O'CLOCK and the town was so quiet, especially when it came to the word "hello." But Aisling tried to ignore both the watch on her wrist and the doubt in her heart. Tiran had said they'd meet at eight in the main square. He'd be here any moment now.

The mist had stopped as the day faded into evening, and the air was dark and still. Only the occasional car or bike passed through the square in the city center. People would occasionally walk past Aisling, and she would return their silent nods.

We all know each other here, she thought, *but they don't really know me at all. My very nature means I can influence their thoughts, feelings, and actions with barely a word. We all get on well enough, but would we if they understood what I am, what I can do?*

The sheer power of the Awen still scared her sometimes. *So much of what I do,* she thought, *is about how little I do. It's easy to influence but hard to make sure I do only what is absolutely needed. All things still must be up to them, not to me. I'm just a steward, a caretaker, a guardian. I nudge, but the only thing I control is myself. Such a vast power, to know that the very will of the world runs through me.*

Am I worthy of this power?

Aisling stared at The Salt and Crane, which stood on the far side of the square. The walking stick lay in its hiding place there, protected from harm yet waiting to be stolen. And who was the thief? Was it Jay? Was it Tiran? Was it someone neither she nor Connemara had yet suspected? Would this be the undoing of them all?

She knew little of the man who had owned the relics, though it was said that he had been ancient, with a lifespan akin to mountains. He'd fled from India with his wife and son, back before India was India or Ireland was Ireland—back before anywhere really had Official Names. His own name had been lost to history, and not even Grandmother had known it.

He himself was said to have died in The Blast, and only his goblet, stick, and box had survived. Aisling knew he brewed the black beer he drank from his goblet, the stout that in time would become Galway Pradesh Stout, the most popular beer in the world.

Stick in hand, he roamed the country around Galway and Clifden. He found the first sacred places, where the world's dreams seeped into reality. From dreams had come seeing. From seeing had come understanding. From understanding had come action. And how he had acted. He helped to bring forth all of them, the Awens, The Management, the Jakes and Jades, the Brewers, the Mimeauxflage...

Aisling's thoughts turned to the cave, far up in the Twelve Bens. The little sandalwood box slept there. In that box he had carried the first barley to Ireland. To this day, the barley's descendants remained the main ingredient of Galway Pradesh Stout.

The goblet, the stick, and the box—all possessed unusual powers because of the man who had carried them. They were just simple everyday items, but if Aisling had learned anything it was that the world's greatest powers always lay in the mundane.

Even though the relics were hidden, they attracted people. The power seeped out into the world like a whisper in the wind, a legend told down the pub after a few pints. For the right man or woman, sooner or later the story did more than whisper. It shouted. It took hold. And when that happened, that person always came to Clifden, trying to find the relics.

It wasn't because of the objects themselves. That always chilled Aisling's blood a little. No, the objects on their own were just a goblet, a stick and a box. When combined and called forth in the sacred place hidden in the Twelve Bens, said the legend, they became so much more. They gave the bearer the power to control the world.

It's never happened, Aisling thought. *My job, the Awen's job, has always been to stop them before it comes to that. To get them to change not just their actions but their intentions. To help them see beyond their need for power and control. Sometimes it worked. But if it didn't...*

Connemara had first taken her to the sacred place in the Bens. When she saw what lined the corridor beyond the entrance, she had nearly fainted—

"Aisling?"

Tiran's smile could've convinced the evening to bring back the sun and go out for a night on the town. A flush came to Aisling's cheeks. The evening wasn't nearly as cool as it had felt moments ago.

"I'm sorry if I made you wonder," he said. "I miscalculated getting back here in time."

"What were you doing?"

He shrugged and offered her his arm. "In comparison, nothing of importance."

"I did start to wonder."

"You had every right to."

She kissed him. "Well, so far so good," she said. "Where to?"

"I thought we'd wander up to that wee cafe you told me about."

"The one on the far side of town?"

"That's the one." Tiran looked ahead and raised his hand.

A taxi pulled up and Tiran opened the door for Aisling. She started to step inside, but a glimpse of The Salt and Crane made her stop.

Flames shot out of the second level. The pub level.

Connemara's level.

"The pub's on fire," she said, closing the taxi door and grabbing Tiran's hand. "We have to help." *No,* she thought. *No no no. This can't be an accident or a coincidence. It's the second relic. Jay's gone for it—*

"There's nothing we can do, and you'd get hurt," Tiran replied. "Besides, the fire department will be here any moment."

"Jake may be hurt," she said. "And who knows how many people are inside." A hot wind of guilt blew through her. *I was so angry with him,* she thought. *What if he's hurt, or worse, and the last thing I told him was how I never wanted to see him again? This wasn't what I meant...*

Some discussion seemed to go on behind Tiran's eyes. "Then come on," he said and started running.

Aisling ran with him. The flames had grown bigger now. Despite the darkness, she could make out the plumes of smoke pouring out of the pub thicker and thicker. Fire boiled out of the top of the building—*Jay's room,* she thought. *What if he's there too? What if they're both...*

Her eyes felt hot and wet. As they neared the burning building, police cars and fire trucks pulled up. *Why would I be sad about Jay anyway?* she thought.

"Get back, Aisling!" shouted a fireman.

If Jay does himself in this time, all the better for the world, Aisling thought. *But what if stopping Jay means losing Jake too?*

She stared at the burning building, eyes wide. "Jake!" she yelled. "Connemara!"

"Everyone down!"

Aisling froze. Her eyes locked on the flames boiling and flaring behind the windows of the bottom floor, the restaurant level.

The glass exploded.

So sharp, so jagged, so fast, the shards flew toward her. She could count the flickering of the firelights winking off the glass. One, two, three, four, die—

A hand grabbed the back of her coat. Flat on her back, the glass still winked orange, red, and yellow as it flew past where she had been standing. *It could have killed me,* she thought. *So who saved me?*

"Are you okay?"

Tiran sat up and ran his hands over her face, her hands, her—

"Watch it," Aisling said.

"You're not hurt," Tiran replied. "Thank goodness." He nodded toward the window, where the firefighters aimed their hoses at the flames pouring out. "You didn't move. I had to pull you down."

Aisling gripped his hand. "I think you just saved my life."

"Over here," someone nearby shouted. "Medics! Bring a stretcher!"

Aisling scrambled to her feet and ran toward the voice. She was much closer now to the fire. She heard coughing and she began to cough. A man kneeled over another man, but Aisling couldn't see their faces. She only heard the fireman behind the kneeling man, saying, "You can move now, son. We've got him." The fireman gently moved the man away. "You have to let us work now."

Tears and blood streaked down Jay's face as he stared, eyes wide, at the man on the pavement between him and Aisling. Jake Connemara was so covered in blood, soot, and burns that Aisling could barely recognize him.

"Is he breathing?" Aisling said, dropping to her knees next to him and the medics.

"Connemara," she said, grabbing his hand. "Jake. Please breathe. Please."

Jake didn't stir when Aisling's tears fell onto his face. He didn't squeeze her hand. The fireman gently brought Aisling to her feet and walked her over to Jay. Then the fireman was where Aisling had been, kneeling by Jake. Neither she nor Jay could see what was happening. They just heard the men swear and saw them moving frantically.

But Jake just lay there, so still, so very still, so very much too still.

"I HEARD JAKE SHOUTING," Jay said, his voice so soft that Aisling could barely hear him. "I never heard anyone else, though. One moment there was yelling. Then there wasn't."

"You make it sound like the pub wasn't open," Aisling said.

"It wasn't," Jay replied. "The stair lights were off. Plus, a note on the door said the pub was closed tonight. Something about busted taps."

"What happened next?"

"I was worried about Jake. Clearly something wasn't right. I ran up the stairs. When I got to the landing, the pub door opened. I couldn't see the person's face, but whoever it was, he got me good. When I came to, I was back at the bottom of the stairs, only on my arse."

"Was the fire going by then?

Jay nodded.

"You could've just run," Aisling said. "Saved yourself."

"No, I couldn't," Jay replied. "You don't let people die when you can do something about it."

"Your pack probably didn't survive this one."

Jay just shrugged. "That'd be a first."

Before Aisling could ask what he was referring to, the fireman came over, his face tired and grave. "He came to," the fireman said. "Barely. He's weak. We have to get him to hospital, but he insisted on seeing you first." The fireman turned to Jay. "You're lucky to be alive, and you gave him a damn sight more luck than he would have had if you hadn't risked your life. The medics will look you over. Then the police need to speak with you."

Jay went where the fireman pointed. Aisling let the fireman lead her to the ambulance, where Jake lay on a stretcher, waiting to be lifted inside.

"I'm sorry," Aisling said. "About everything."

"Dangerous," Jake said. His voiced faded in and out. He turned his head so she could see him better. His pupils were different sizes. "Most in the world... You must be more careful than ever." Some of the black was gone from his face now. Aisling tried not to think too much about the nature of the bumps and shadows that remained. "He's not who he says he is. He's dangerous. He nearly killed me. He's killed a Jake before."

"Who did this?" Aisling said. "Jay told me his

version, and Tiran was with me. I don't know who to believe."

"The name he gave you is not his real name," Jake said. "What he gives to you, he does not give for you."

"Who is it? Jay? Tiran? Someone else?"

Jake's head rolled to one side, his eyes closed. His chest stuttered up and down.

Two medics came up to the stretcher. Aisling tried to make out who they were, but something about their faces made it seem like they could be both anyone and no one. "We have to take him now," one of the medics said.

The other medic stared at her. "Did he tell you what he needed to say?"

Aisling squeezed Jake's hand. "I don't know," she replied. "Will he be okay?

The other medic shrugged. Soon the ambulance was gone.

Aisling stared at the building. She could see that the flames were nearly under control, but she didn't need to see the hidden compartment in the wall to know the stick had been taken. She didn't need to see it swinging from Jay's hand. *Or Tiran's,* she thought. *I owe it to Jake to remember what he said.*

Two relics stolen. Leaving only the box. Leaving only one relic between what was and the horror of what could be.

Jay and Tiran were on opposite ends of the

scene, each being questioned by the police. Another officer came over to her. "Evening, Davey," Aisling said.

"We'll figure out what happened, Aisling," he replied. "And let's keep it to 'Sergeant' tonight, okay?"

She nodded. "Sorry."

"I know you and ole Connemara are close."

"He's like family," she replied. "Makes me feel all the worse. Like family, I said some nasty things to him earlier."

"He'll pull through," said the sergeant, his voice flat. "If he really is like family, though, he'll forgive you."

Aisling tried to smile. "I guess you need to get a statement from me now?"

When they finished he said, "I don't think for a moment this was an accident. Those two blokes from elsewheres, I don't know about them."

"That makes two of us."

"That one you're stepping out with lately—"

"Oy."

He shrugged. "That's hardly a denial. But he seems okay. Was he with you when you saw the flames?"

She nodded.

"That leaves the other," said the sergeant. "Jay, he says his name is."

"Is it?"

"His passport matches, but you know how things are nowadays." The sergeant leaned in close and tapped his nose with a finger. "Those things can be faked."

"Jay said he was knocked out by someone who'd been arguing with Jake."

"Aye, that's what he says."

"Do you suspect..."

"Don't know anything yet. And certainly nothing that would have us lock either of them up till we do. But stay sharp, Aisling." He patted her shoulder. "And keep an eye on that one," he said, pointing to Jay. "He seems to me like he's hiding something. I'm itching to find out what."

The sergeant walked away.

Time started to blur. The firemen put the fire out. Aisling overheard mention of an empty compartment in the pub wall, but that was no surprise.

Nothing else got her attention until someone walked out from the building carrying Jay's backpack.

"Looks like it fell through the floor," the fireman said. "All the way down. Talk about lucky." He handed the unscathed pack to Jay, and Aisling walked over.

"Where will you be staying now?" Aisling asked.

Jay shrugged.

"Come on to the hostel," Aisling replied.

"Maybe that's not a good idea," Jay said. "Seems like everywhere I go around here, bad things happen." He stared hard at her. "Aisling, you know I didn't have anything to do with this, right? Not the hostel, not the pub, not Jake."

"I know," she said, her voice soft. "It's just bad luck."

"Yeah, I've got tons of that apparently." The gleam was gone from his eye.

"You'll stay at the hostel tonight," Aisling said. "No charge. Consider it a favor."

Jay nodded. "Thank you."

Besides, that stick is harder to hide, she thought. *If you have it, I'll find you out. Then we'll see what you really think of Clifden.*

Tiran came over. "Oh. Hi, Jay," he said.

"Tiran."

The chill passing between the two men could've put out the fire in moments.

"Heard you were pretty heroic back there," Tiran said.

"Heard you kept Aisling from getting hurt," Jay replied.

"I hope everything worked out for you," Tiran said.

Jay stared at him. "I wish I knew what you were talking about."

Tiran grinned.

An officer came over. "Aisling," he said, "do you

need a lift?"

"Do you mind taking us all to the hostel?"

As they went to the police car, Aisling puzzled over all that had happened, the sudden hostility between the two men, and Connemara's strange words.

I have to figure this out, she thought. *One more relic, and this all gets much, much worse.*

"WHAT DO YOU MEAN he's gone?" Aisling said again, clenching the phone tighter to her ear.

"A note was left," the hospital nurse said. "Mr. Connemara has been removed to specialized care in a dedicated facility."

"A note?" Aisling said. "What is this? A hall pass from school?"

"I appreciate you're upset," the nurse said. "But it was signed 'The Management.' Everything was done quite correctly. I'm sure contact details will be made available to you at the appropriate time. Now, if you'll excuse me."

The line went dead.

Aisling made a cuppa tea. She'd just added the milk when Tiran came up to the front counter. "Rough morning?" he asked.

"I've had better."

He nodded. "I know the feeling." He leaned in close. "Look, I know this may not be the best timing. But you've had a hard time, and I wanted to help you feel better."

Aisling sipped her tea. "I'm listening."

"Would you be willing to go on a walk with me this afternoon? I want to give you something."

He could be the thief, Aisling thought. *So charming. So smooth. Or he could just be amazing. An equal. Someone I can open up to. Someone I can feel excited to be with. Either way...*

She smiled. "Okay."

"I'll meet you here around four." Tiran grinned. "And I promise I'll be on time."

They wandered out into the Irish morning, where the mist was lighter than the sun. She kissed Tiran gently.

I hate to see you go, Aisling thought. She stared more closely. *But I love to watch you leave.*

As the morning continued, Aisling tried to work through the day's chores. There were reservations to check, money to count, a kitchen to tidy—

No, she thought. *Strike that last one. That's still a ways off...*

But no matter what she did or how hard she worked, her mind ran and ran. Rumors of a powerful object stolen from The Blast Memorial. Two charming men who show up the same day. Two fires. A Jake nearly dying. The test of the new Awen of Ireland...

The relics weren't anywhere near the two men's

bags or beds. Which made sense; if one or both of them had the wherewithal to steal the relics, they wouldn't be stupid enough to leave them where Aisling could find them, but she knew she still had to check.

Jay or Tiran? she thought. *Tiran or Jay?*

Aisling had just poured a late-afternoon cuppa when Jay came into the hostel. Nervousness shone like sweat on the backpacker.

Guilt? she thought. *Was nearly killing Connemara too much for you? But if you want the relics and the power that comes through them, surely some naff bartender wouldn't be something to get upset about...*

"Oh. Hi, uh, Aisling. Hi," Jay stammered. "Sorry," he continued, shaking his head. "At least I didn't call you Ashley, though, huh?"

Aisling sighed. "Something I can help you with?"

Jay took off his daypack and set it on the counter between them. "Look, these last few days have been hard on you. And while I don't know what you're upset with me about, that doesn't really matter. I just want you to know I hope you're okay. Meeting you has been the best thing to happen to me during all my time on the road. Or off it, really. I wanted to give you something." He reached into the pack and took out a badly folded, rumpled brown T-shirt.

He set it in front of her and smiled.

Aisling looked away. *This can't happen,* she thought. *This has to be done.*

She set the bundled shirt back on the counter and slid it toward him. "I can't accept anything you want to give me."

"But I—"

"I know. And I won't disagree. You're attracted to me. And I'm attracted to you. In another life, maybe there could've been something." Aisling shook her head. "But we're not in another life. In this life, you are you—whoever that is. And I am I. Clifden doesn't want you here." She paused and bit her lip. "And neither do I."

"I'm still trying."

"And you're still failing." Anger washed through her and roared from her mind to her mouth. "Dammit, Jay. Don't you understand at all? The reason you can't find a job or a place to stay? That reason is me. I told people not to rent to you. I told people not to hire you."

"You..."

"Me. All of it. Right down to the melting breakfast."

Redness flooded Jay's face. He opened his mouth but closed it. His shoulders sagged and he looked from her to the floor. All the fight, all the strength fell out of him. "Okay," he said, looking at her with eyes dull as the winter's grayest sky. "I guess you and Clifden get what you want." He shook his head. "I just wish it had been me."

Without another word, Jay took the bundled

shirt, put it back in his daypack, and walked away. A few minutes later, he left the hostel, his backpack on his back. He didn't look at Aisling. He didn't say a word. He just left. When the door closed behind him, Aisling took a deep breath and exhaled slowly.

About time, she thought. *Maybe this first test won't be so bad after all.*

She looked at the clock and smiled. Time to get ready to meet Tiran.

WHEN THEY WERE ALL but among the first clefts of the hills, Aisling and Tiran paused at the top of a small crest on the path to the Twelve Bens. The mountain was closer too, but looking at it just confused Aisling. Jay was gone, but the mountain still looked angry.

"I've never met anyone like you," Tiran said. "Do you ever get tired?" He adjusted the straps of the small daypack on his back.

"I'm just a wee woman who runs a hostel," Aisling replied. "And I've walked these hills since I was a girl. We're used to each other."

"The way you move, it's like you're part of each other." Tiran looked out over the hills. Late sunlight filtered through the patchy clouds and lit up the Bens. "You really love it here, don't you?"

"I learned to," Aisling said. "There was a time when I was eager to be away. For a long time, I was."

"What made you come back?"

"I saw things that scared me. Things that weren't your usual bits of boring ole life. It was like I'd scratched the skin of the world—our dull, tired, dirty world—and beneath all that I found something I didn't expect."

"What did you find?"

She smiled and looked from Tiran to the hills. "There was something shining. Something beautiful. Something that made me understand things as I'd never understood them before." She looked back at Tiran and saw him staring enthralled and wide-eyed at the bright patch of gold and green he had pulled from his pants pocket.

Is that what he's going to give me? she thought. It looked like a necklace. He hadn't noticed her looking. She glanced away and turned to him again only when he'd put the gift back in his pocket. "I came home after that," Aisling said. "Out of all the places in the world, I understood that this one was the best for me."

"Maybe you'll tell me the whole story sometime," Tiran said.

"Well, I'll show you mine if you show me yours," Aisling replied, grinning. "You've never exactly gone into detail yourself."

"I suppose not. Similar reasons too. Sometimes it's still too hard for me to believe that what happened actually happened," Tiran said. "It's so easy to think of how dull and mundane the world must be. But it's not. There are powers and wonders beyond all our imaginations, and they are just as real as sunrise and sunset." He stepped close to her. "Maybe that's what draws us together so powerfully, Aisling. It's like around each other we know we're not alone. We know there's someone who understands."

She laid her hand on his chest and drew her face toward his. But as she started to close her eyes, he stepped back.

"Wow." Wonder lit up his face as he looked at something behind her. "What's that?" he said and then ran.

"Tiran?" Aisling ran too, but he was faster, much faster, and she could barely see him. A moment later, the clefts of the hills concealed him, and it was as if Tiran had never been there at all.

Where did he go? she thought. *What did he see?*

A haze fell away from her mind and she saw it too. From where they had been standing, the black gaping cave must have looked like an open mouth. That's what it reminded her of, at least. Whenever she was inside, it always made her want to scream.

He's got to be going to the cave, she thought. *And if he's going to the cave, then he's not who I thought he was. He has the first two relics, and now he's going for the third.*

Aisling ran.

She neared a bend. The path before her was obscured by a large rock outcropping. She stepped around. There was a blur, something like a *thrum*, and a flash. Then there was the sky above her, gray and blurry. Beneath her, cold ground and rocks dug into her back.

Then nothing at all.

From the darkness came a light, bright and blinding. Then there was darkness again. And pain. Her left temple throbbed. When she felt how swollen it was, more pain shot through her skull.

Aisling shook her head and opened her eyes. Darkness. Cool, smooth stone beneath her. Slightly damp air.

The cave.

Fear pulsed through her.

"It's very difficult," came the voice in the dark, "to hit someone in the temple just hard enough to make them unconscious, but not so hard that you kill them."

"Do you want a feckin medal then?" she replied.

"A box will do just fine."

The light came back, shining in her eyes. She screamed, scrambled up to her feet.

The light swung away, and she could see nothing again. But she could hear. Something was scrabbling across the floor of the cave, coming closer, getting louder—

Something bounced off the toes of her shoes.

"You'll need a flashlight."

I'm not tied up, she thought. *Maybe I can blind him and make a run for it.* She reached down and picked up the light. When she went to click the switch, the other light blinded her again.

"I know what you're thinking. How about hearing me out first?"

A *psssst* sound made her jump, and Aisling clicked on her light.

Tiran stood behind a large, waist-high rock. He pointed the flashlight up toward his face, as if he were about to tell a scary story around a campfire. He was swathed in strange shadows, and she couldn't see his eyes—only black pools. In his other hand, he held a can of Galway Pradesh Stout and he poured it into—

"The goblet," she said. "You."

"Of course," Tiran replied. "I can't say I'm displeased that you thought it was Jay. Made things much easier, that's for sure. But I did think you were smarter than that, Aisling. Or do you prefer Awen?"

Tiran crushed the empty can and threw it over his shoulder. He picked up the goblet and raised it toward her with a nod. "To the Awen of Ireland!" he said, taking a long drink of stout. "Wow. I bet this old cup could make piss taste like a good martini." When he set the goblet down, she saw the walking stick, thin and slender on the flat boulder.

Aisling touched her temple.

"Yes," Tiran said. "I'm afraid so. Punching a lady isn't very gentlemanly. I thought it best to use what I had at hand, and there's nothing like a good stick." He took another drink of stout. "As you know, the relics are quite powerful."

"They didn't tell you who I was, though."

"No," Tiran replied. "Your friend Jake did that."

"Jake would never."

"Oh, fine. You're right. It's not like I tortured him or something. Besides, I've learned enough of Jakes and Jades to know how hard they are to kill." Tiran smiled. "Not impossible, by any stretch. But damn hard."

"You didn't kill him."

"For now. Once you've killed one Jake, it's hard to feel sated. It's like eating only one chip."

"He'll recover. No matter what you do to me, he'll find you. They'll all find you."

"Of course they will." Tiran chuckled. "I really did think you were smarter than this."

Stay focused, Aisling thought. *I'm still alive, and he doesn't have the box yet.*

"I must admit, learning about you was a lucky stroke." He reached into his pocket and took out the necklace.

"Much as I appreciate you wanting to give me something," Aisling said, "I think you'll understand if I respectfully decline."

"Give you this?" Tiran laughed. "It's worth three of you. But every time I was near you, it's like it went haywire. It's like the necklace can sniff out power, you see. It made it easy to find the first relic. The second was more difficult. The cave was such a different place that it stuck out to me, and I figured the third relic must be here. There had to be a reason. I figured having you along would make it more likely that nothing unfortunate would happen to me."

"You stole the necklace from The Blast Memorial."

Tiran nodded. "Ah, they questioned me hard too. Searched my pack. Turned out my pockets. Made me take off my boots, even. He wiggled his left foot. But they never thought to look at the bottom of my sock. I don't know all the necklace's secrets yet. It's old. It resists me. But in time, I'll understand it even better than I understand you."

"I'm touched you wanted to get to know me so closely."

"Jake did make it easier that night. I'd snuck in earlier, broken all the tap lines so the pub would have to be closed, then just waited. I thought he'd left, but he came back just as I'd taken out the walking stick. But I had the element of surprise on my side—and, well, a stick. It was only by good luck that I saw the letter at the back of the bar. He hadn't finished it yet. You must have said some terrible things to have him trying so hard to get back into your good graces. He'd written enough to tell me all I needed to know about you. He said you're the avatar of the world. Muse to those who live and yearn. Protector." Tiran shook his head and sighed. "Well, maybe two out of three isn't bad."

"What happened to all the wonders of the world?" Aisling asked. "You talked as if you love the world, as if you have high regard for life. But you don't."

"I lost that a long time ago, along with some other things I didn't need anymore."

Aisling remembered something Connemara had said. "Is Tiran your real name? What kind of a name is that, anyway?"

"It's my chosen one," Tiran replied. "Much better than a given one." He leaned forward. In the yellow light of the flashlights, his smile seemed both sickly and like a flame. "If it helps, if it makes you feel better, I used to be known as Declan."

Aisling leaned forward too. "Sometimes not even a good Irish name is enough to take the eejit out of someone," she said. She whipped the beam of her light up so it shone into Tiran's eyes, then threw the flashlight so it cracked off his temple. He crumpled to the floor. The flashlight hit the ground, and the light winked out, leaving her in darkness.

She stepped to where he had been, her hands reaching and grabbing. Finally, she found the stick. More scrabbling. More reaching in the dark. Beer slopped as she grabbed the goblet. Run one way, and I can make a stand where the third relic is. *No, she thought. That won't do. Get out of here. Flee into the hills. Head back to the hostel. Whatever it takes. Just get these away from the third. Get them away from here.*

"Memorize this place," Grandmother had told her via Connemara when he'd first brought her here three years earlier. "Know every rock, every bump on the ground, on the sides, over your head. Know every turn and straight. Know it so you could run it blind and in the dark."

I'm about to find out.

Aisling took off toward the mouth of the cave.

Rounding corners and bends, Aisling swerved left at just the right moment and felt the air change as she ran past the stalactite hanging down where her head would have been. The cave felt close and tight. Panic rose in her, but she fought it back down.

She ran through a thin opening. Rock scraped her shoulders as she passed. The air immediately changed. She came to a larger, longer tunnel, and she stopped for a moment to get her breath and to listen. Silence behind her.

And before her, The Warning.

Connemara had said it was called that for a simple reason; those who came for the relics had to have a chance to change their ways. To turn back. The Warning was just that: their last chance.

What better warning could there be than to see what had happened when those who came before you had not turned back?

A beam of light lit up a face. For a moment, Aisling saw the hands beside the head, the chains around the wrists, the frozen scream—all behind a layer of stone so thin it was skin-like. The light made the stone layer cloudy.

The light, she thought. *How could a light be shining there? Unless—*

She ran. There was one last turn beyond The Warning. Then she would reach the mouth of the cave, then fresh air, freedom, then a chance, a chance—

Something heavy slammed into her back. She fell face first, flat onto the floor of the cave, surrounded by those who had tried, those who had failed.

The air rushed out of her, and she coughed, trying to breathe. A bright beam of light blinded her.

"Sometimes a lad just doesn't get to finish his beer," he said. "Back to where we came."

"You might as well kill me."

"Ah, but I do like you," said Tiran. "The kisses were nice."

"I won't help you."

"You will. If you don't, once I combine the relics, once I take the power that is mine, then the very first thing I'll do is find Jay. I'll bring him back here, and I will kill him slowly until all that's left of him is a scream. And I'll make you watch. I'll probably even find ways to make you help." Tiran smiled. "Once I'm done with Jay, I'll do the same to every person in Clifden—every man, every woman, every child. But if you help me now, I'll leave all of them alone."

Tiran tucked the goblet into the small daypack, lashed the stick to the outside of it, and put the pack on his back. With the hand that wasn't holding the flashlight he grabbed Aisling's arm, pulled her to her feet, and led her back into the depths of the cave.

I'm sorry, Jay, she thought, as her breath slowly came back. *I should've trusted you more. I should've known all along.*

"Points for a solid throw," Tiran said. "You nearly knocked me out. I was actually woozy for a moment there. See what I mean, though? It's hard to get it just right." He motioned to the passage that began past the boulder. "I believe you know the way, Awen. Ladies first."

They followed the short passage to the edge. She closed her eyes as she stood there with her toes hanging off into space.

Tiran stopped just behind her. "Well, Aisling," he said, "you lot do have style."

She opened her eyes. The shock of all the light made it hard to see at first, but her eyes adjusted quickly. The flashlight beam reflected off the thousands of crystals that covered the ceiling and the walls of the large cavern. At the center, a long, thin stalactite pointed down to the middle of the chamber.

Below them, below the stalactite, a small sandalwood box sat on a short pedestal of rock.

Tiran nudged her in the ribs. "It's time to get this over with. Down you go."

Aisling turned and lowered herself onto the ancient ladder-like steps that had been cut into the stone. Tiran followed her down, hopping off just before she got her footing on the floor. He was standing stable and ready before she could have done anything.

"Didn't you want to give me something?" Aisling asked.

"What?"

"When you asked me to go on a walk with you. Did you actually want to give me something, or was that just a ruse?"

"Oh, yes, that," Tiran said. He stared at the stalactite and the pedestal, and frowned. "In a moment, though. Gifts are best when they're reciprocal, after all. You give me one first." He smiled. "Then I'll return the favor."

Aisling smiled. "All right."

With every step, she stared not at the box but at the stalactite. *Will it matter that I'm the Awen?* she thought. *Will the trap spring for me? He senses it. That's why he's making me take it and not him. But I don't know what will happen. Grandmother certainly never had any stories about this...*

Tiran followed her step for step. He was so close that she could feel his breath on the back of her neck.

They stood at the pedestal.

"Go ahead," Tiran said. "Take it. Remember what I said about Jay, about everyone you've ever known. Slowly. And you'll not only watch. You'll help. I'll kill them—but I'll drive you mad."

The scent of sandalwood still passed into her, refreshing and soothing.

Punch him. Run. Do something. He can't hurt anyone, but he doesn't know that.

Tiran slapped her. As her vision reeled, he grabbed the box from the pedestal and jumped backward. In her disorientation, Aisling stayed where she was.

The stalactite plunged down, piercing the pedestal. All around Aisling, crystal rods erupted from the cave floor, rising just above her head and then angling and forming a ceiling. With a flash, the crystal fused into a solid mass, enclosing her like a vertical coffin.

On the other side of the crystal, Tiran waved at her. "I suppose you can guess," he said. "Not that it's a surprise. My gift to you is death. Good-bye, Aisling." He held up the box, smiled, and walked away.

Aisling took a deep breath and closed her eyes. Tears wanted to come, but she made herself breathe, breathe, breathe. *Maybe this is what's supposed to happen to an Awen who fails,* she thought. *At least no one will say I cried at the end.*

Upon hearing the sound, she opened her eyes. Water poured down the walls of the crystal box so quickly it soaked her shoes and rose over her knees, her hips, her shoulders.

The light dimmed. *Tiran's left,* she thought. *He'll be in the other chamber soon enough. Then it all ends.*

The last light went out. In the darkness, Aisling closed her eyes and kept the tears at bay. She breathed in deeply as the water rose past her chin.

There's not even anyone to miss me, she thought. *Grandmother, Mum, Dad—they're all gone. Not Jay, not anymore. Maybe Connemara. If he's even still alive...*

I'll die alone, she thought. *The broken Awen... the failed Awen...*

Her thoughts faded as her need for breath grew.

The water covered her, and she opened her eyes.

It doesn't matter whether or not I cry, she thought.

The tears drown too.

III

THE LIGHT SEEMED so far away that she could never reach it.

Then the light was coming to her instead. A silver-gold brilliance surrounded Aisling.

Will Grandmother be waiting for me? Will Mum and Dad? Or will I be abandoned?

A cracking sound filled her. At the sound, the light seemed no closer than before, but she was falling, falling...

Cold. Wet. Where was the light?

"Aisling?"

The voice was warm, but there couldn't be any warmth here. Not for an Awen who had failed—

"Aisling?"

Water had been everywhere. She'd tried to keep it out, but the water had gotten into her too. It had chased out the air. It had chased out the life. But now Aisling felt the water rise out of her stomach and lungs, pouring over her and splashing on the floor.

Hands were on her face, then on her back, lifting her up so she sat.

More water and more water and more water. Her throat felt raw and hot, but the coughing subsided, and the air was coming back, the sweet air.

Aisling opened her eyes.

Every muscle in his face seemed taut to the point of snapping. The cavern had darkened, but his green-gold eyes blazed in the dim light. He held a small flashlight.

"Jay?" She coughed in pain. The spasms doubled her over as the last of the water sputtered out.

Jay held onto her, waiting. "You really know how to scare the hell out of a guy, you know that?"

She put her hands on the floor and sat up straighter. Something sharp poked her palm. She picked up a piece of thin, jagged, translucent crystal.

"If you want to know how I got you out of that crystal phone box of death," Jay said, "I honestly don't know. I can't say I like what you did to me, but that doesn't mean you should die or that I'd leave you to die. I don't know how long I pounded on that thing, but it's like I forgave you, and once I did, the crystal cracked. Moments later, the whole thing shattered, and there you were."

His knuckles were red, cracked, and bleeding. "You came looking for me?" Aisling said.

"Even when I meant to leave Clifden, I still ended up at that damn sign," Jay said. "But no India or Idaho this time. Just one arrow that said 'Aisling, The Cave of The Warning.' That didn't exactly sound good, so I legged it to the hostel and dumped my big pack. I was trying to figure out where this cave was when I heard two guys say you and Tiran had headed toward the Bens. From there I just ran, saw the cave from the path, and figured that had to be it."

He swung his daypack off his shoulders. "You're soaked," Jay said, reaching inside the pack and pulling out the same crumpled brown bundle from earlier. "At least let's get a dry shirt on you."

Something clinked on the floor as Aisling unfolded the shirt, which she held up to read the front. "'Tea,'" she said, "'It's Just Not Coffee.'"

Jay blushed. "Had a bloke at the shirt shop in town make it for me. It's... it's what I was going to give you earlier. Something to remember me by. Well, partly that."

Aisling reached down to where she had heard the clink. Even in the dim light, she recognized the knots and curves of the long, thick silver necklace.

Known as "The Renewal," the pattern had come to symbolize all the striving, rebirth, and inspiration that had come out of The Blast.

"It seemed like it was perfect for you," Jay said.

"Thank you," she said. "Thank you for everything." She put on the necklace. Some warmth seemed to pass into her as the pattern touched her skin. Jay closed his eyes while she changed shirts. "I'm sorry," she said. "I was wrong, Jay. It was Tiran all along."

"Tiran... what? Why?"

Fear rose in Aisling's eyes. She grabbed Jay's hand. "It's complicated, and it's about to get much worse. I promise I will tell you everything later. Well, if we make it out alive."

Jay ran and Aisling ran too, though her lungs screamed at her. *He's with me,* she thought. *After all I did to him. After I betrayed his trust. He's following me, even though he doesn't even understand what he's gotten himself into.*

Side by side, they crossed the cavern. "What are we going to do?" Jay asked.

"Tiran has tracked down three sacred relics. The third was hidden where you found me. He is taking them all to a place of great power." Aisling pointed to a dark spot at the far end of the crystal cavern. "With the combined relics, he will gain an ultimate power. A power to control the world."

"So, Grand World Master Tiran?"

"Yes."

Jay ran faster. "Bugger that."

Aisling smiled and matched his pace.

They stopped as they reached the passage, and she squeezed his hand. "Jay," Aisling said, "this won't be easy. I can't promise we'll survive."

"You nearly died already, and you're still going forward," Jay replied. "So I will too. Besides, this is bigger than just you and me."

They walked quietly. After reaching a bend, a red-orange light brought a dim, bloody glow. Jay turned off his light and followed Aisling into a small chamber. At the back wall, Tiran looked down at a smooth, black rock that had been carved into a rough block. The front had been inscribed with the outlines of a goblet, a box, and a stick. Combined just so, they looked like a triangle.

"What are those?" Jay asked. "Instructions?"

"Every weapon has a manual," Aisling replied, a thin grimness in her voice. "Maybe there's a chance. One final chance."

Tiran looked up from the block. Before him, the stick was lying parallel to the width of the block. In front of it was the sandalwood box, and in front of that was the goblet. The eerie red-orange light began to pulse and flicker. As it did, Tiran's smile grew bigger until his mouth seemed to be made of shadow and flame.

"You're too late," Tiran said. "The relics are mine.

They are one again. Now I claim the power that is mine, and with that I claim the world!"

The lights pulsed faster, and the relics glowed silver and gold. Tiran stretched out his arms and threw back his head, as the light from the relics engulfed him.

AISLING LAUGHED. The light faded, withdrawing from Tiran and back into the relics like water draining away.

Jay took his hand away from his eyes. "Um, Aisling."

"Yes?"

"Where did the chains come from?"

Tiran looked left and then right. He began to struggle. Thick black shackles fastened around his wrists, waist and ankles, and they pulled him backward until he was drawn taut against the wall of the chamber. The chains clinked taut with one final tug, and Tiran gasped.

"Oh, those," Aisling said, as nonchalantly as if she'd been pointing out a tea kettle. "All part of the light show."

"What is this?" Tiran shouted with rage burning in his eyes. "Where is my power?"

Aisling walked over to the block and ran her hand over the relics. "It's a shame you poured out that beer," she said. "I could do with a pint right now." She looked up and met Tiran's gaze. "I really didn't want this to happen. We never do. Though, since you wanted to kill me, I can't say I feel sorry for you anymore."

Jay looked from Tiran to Aisling. "It's a dupe, isn't it?" he said. "It's like those street games with the three coconut shells and the pea. You're so certain you can find the pea that you keep betting and betting and betting. But you can never find the pea. The guys running the game palm it every go, while you just bleed money."

"I heard the stories," Tiran said. "And the necklace. Its power showed me. It took me to the relics. They have power. This is the place of power."

"That part is all true," Aisling replied. "The stories have some truth to them. They are the relics of an ancient man who had them for much of his life, and they came with him from India to Ireland long ago. And yes, this is a place of power. A trap must be convincing to attract its prey. As to the rest —well, you saw the entryway, Tiran. It's called The Warning for a reason. Do those figures seem more familiar now?"

Tiran glanced again at his hands, which were up near his head. The color fell out of his face. "No," he said.

Aisling nodded. "Yes. The relics, this place, the entire thing is a ruse. A setup. We draw in those who have too great a lust for power. Those who want to rule and ruin the world. People like you, Tiran. We let them prove and reveal the twisting of their natures, the inner flaws, the choices that drive them to such horrible ends. But here's the thing. The really terrible thing. You could have turned back. Each one of the people in The Warning? They could have turned back too. Many do. Over the years, many people saw the wrongness in their ways, and they gave up this pursuit. They changed. They became better people. They lived full lives of love, achievement, giving, instead of having mad existences, lusting for power and domination."

"The ones in the entryway," Jay said. "They didn't change their minds."

"No. They got all the way here. Though admittedly, Tiran, none have ever been so destructive as you. Most use nothing but stealth and speed. The fires, the near-murder... You certainly raised the bar. Once you proved you wouldn't turn back, the trap sprang."

"What becomes of me?"

"Your body will be suspended in the rock," Aisling said. "You will become part of The Warning."

"Alive?"

"Of course not. You die, though I suppose you could think of it as living on as a sculpture," Aisling said. "If it's any consolation, you'll do more good in death than you did in life."

"What of redemption and mercy?" Tiran asked. "Do I not receive a chance to mend my ways?"

"I know," Aisling said. "That's always what happens in movies and pulp novels and what-not. The big bad villain always gets another second chance. I guess the lesson is supposed to be that the difference between the hero and the villain is that the hero always gives an opportunity for the villain to redeem himself." Aisling smiled. "But as my grandmother liked to point out, all those movie producers and book publishers knew that the villain had to be able to come back so people would see the next film or buy the next book. That's all well and fine for that stuff. But this is real life. There's a world to keep turning. There are lives that need to keep getting on. To want to control the world is to give up your right to live in it."

"You're going to kill me," Tiran said. "How noble."

"I'm not going to kill you," Aisling replied. "You set that destiny on yourself the moment you brought the relics here. I'm just going to see things through."

Tiran leaned forward, his face tight and drawn. His eyes, pale and harsh like a winter fire, burned at both Aisling and Jay. "Then get on with it."

"Just one thing before I do," Aisling said. "Did you care for me at all?"

Jay stared at her, but Tiran smiled and said,

"Wouldn't you just love to know." He settled back against the rock. All the tension faded out of his body. "Stupid woman."

She grinned. "Step back, Jay. This part can be messy."

Jay shuffled back. Tiran sneered. "You think you're so powerful, but you were so easy to mislead."

Aisling stared Tiran in the eyes. "I do make my mistakes," she said. "But I'm the Awen of Ireland. Muse and protector. Seer and guardian. What wrongs are done, I make right. And now, it's time to remove the mistake that was you."

I erred, she thought, *but I have not failed. I was redeemed and restored. I was forgiven and saved.* Aisling held her hands over the relics and closed her eyes.

"Wait," said an impossible voice.

Aisling turned and opened her eyes. *No,* she thought. *It can't be.*

AT THE MOUTH of the passage, fully healed, stood Jake Connemara.

"Connemara?" Aisling said. "But, you, you were... and then you were gone, and..."

"Yes, yes, and yes," Jake replied. "The nurse told you the truth, by the way. Jakes and Jades are very hard to kill. We typically recover from injuries quickly, but Tiran and the fire harmed me beyond my usual abilities. Then again, he has experience. The Management themselves had to recuperate me."

Jay looked back and forth between Jake Connemara and Aisling. "What's going on?" he said. "How did this go from otherworldly weird to completely feckin strange?"

"Don't worry," Jake said. "You are right where we'd hoped you would be."

"Jay was part of my test?"

"The test wasn't only for you, Aisling," Jake replied. "We did fear for you, and you did err greatly, but you found your way again. As for Jay, he has a much larger destiny before him. That's why the mountain is here."

"To make sure he stays on track?"

Jake nodded.

"Sorry," Jay replied, "I don't care much for people telling me where I'm going."

"Oh, don't worry. It doesn't work like that," Jake replied. "Your path is your path. Some destinations are just preferred over others."

"Preferred by you."

"I'm sorry for how condescending this may sound, but one day you'll understand. When that day comes, I'll stand you a pint and we can talk."

"There are bigger things for you than Clifden," Aisling said. "That's why I had to convince you to leave. I have a duty to the world, Jay. As much as I like you, as much as I am glad to have met you, that duty is still more important than anything."

"Excuse me," Tiran said. "I'm so glad you're getting to have this reunion. And congratulations on being restored to your health, Jake. But would you mind getting on with the whole part about killing me? Though listening to all your prattle is so tedious, the boredom may do the job for you."

"That's why we're all here, Tiran," Jake said. "Or rather, Declan. It's your given name, after all."

Tiran snarled.

"Charming," Jake replied. "But Aisling, we're not going to have the usual. Not for him."

"Why not?"

"Something happened to Declan years ago. The Management is partially responsible. The end result is a man who lost his way, who lost all ways. His actions are his, but perhaps if we had done things differently, his actions and intentions would be different too. Declan, we're taking you with us. The Management want to help you. They want to make things right. If we can, we'll restore you to the destiny you lost so long ago. You don't even realize how big a threat you are to life and the world, Declan. But it doesn't have to be this way. You were a good man once. Troubled, but good. We can ease your trouble. We can help you find the good within you again. We can bring you to a peaceful place, a meaningful life in the world."

"If I had any destiny, it died when you took her."

"Well, that's not exactly true. It died when—"

"And my place in the world is whatever I make it," Tiran said, "though I appreciate you reminding me about how I'm freed from your shackles. None of your destiny rules me." A smile grew over his face and he leaned forward.

"No man's destiny can continue once the chains have him," Aisling said.

"Quite effective too," Tiran said. "Shame about that one little flaw."

Jake's face turned pale. "Aisling, get back!"

"After all, I have no destiny," Tiran said. "How can chains hold something that doesn't exist?" A fire seemed to blaze in his eyes as he stretched forward. He clenched his fists and then opened his hands.

The chains shattered. Black fragments blurred fast yet slow.

From the corner of her eye, Aisling saw Jay's head tip back as if he had been punched. A large fragment bounced off his head and flew up into the air. Jay slumped to the floor and did not rise.

Aisling clapped her hand to her neck. She felt the warm, sticky trickle on her throat, but she also felt no metal, only the absence of knots and patterns. *The necklace,* she thought. *If I hadn't been wearing it...*

But there was no time to search the shadows of

the chamber floor. At the mouth of the passage, Jake Connemara's eyes rolled back in his head. He slumped to his knees and fell over, his face and body smacking the rock.

Tiran stepped away from the wall.

All but one of the shackles had cracked and fallen from him. Black metal still clamped around his right wrist, but he paid no mind. He just walked up to the block again. His smile was like a scythe as he held his hands over the relics.

"Destiny is a shackle," he said. "I am the world's first free man." He sneered at Jake's body. "All these years I feared them," Tiran said. "I've run around the world trying to make sure The Management couldn't find me. But they can't hurt me. Not them. Not their Jakes and Jades."

The relics and the trap should have worked, Aisling thought. *But that's just it. Tiran's like nothing we've ever faced.*

She stared at Tiran and she felt her own eyes widen. *There's nothing we can do,* she thought. *Leading him to the relics wasn't like springing a trap. It was like leading him into an armory.*

"You heard what he told you," Aisling said, pleading. "They want to help you."

"You can help yourselves," Tiran replied. "You don't want to help me. My choices were to be frozen in rock or to be taken to The Management. That's not help. You just want to fit me with new chains and some new precious destiny. Please. You act so noble, but it's a sham, a cover-up. You're a lobotomy of the spirit, a castration of the soul. Life is your slave, and nothing scares you more than something out of your control." Tiran smiled. "I am free. I am not yours to command, but you, all the world, will be mine."

"What are you going to do?" Aisling said.

"What I've meant to do all along. Take what is mine."

"How could you even do this? No one has, has ever..."

"I know. You have such a good setup here, such a wonderful game. But that's the thing about games, Awen of Ireland. Games have rules. In your case, those rules are rigged to ensure that you and your precious Management always win." Tiran reached into his pocket. "But that's the thing about me. I don't play by your rules. Not anymore."

Tiran took out the necklace. "Seems such a small trinket," he said. "It's certainly pretty and beautifully designed. That gold was cast so long ago you'd think fire hadn't been discovered yet. And this jade. See this blue-green shimmer to it? That's very rare. It's found only in the Himalayas, in some place called the Heart of the World. Maybe you've heard of it?"

Aisling said nothing but her mind screamed. *Of course I've heard of it,* she thought; *this place draws its power from there. All life, all love, all possibility and striving came from the people who came from there.*

"I've searched for it, of course, but it seems that the more you look for it, the harder it is to find." Tiran shrugged. "No matter. I'll find my way soon enough. Soon, all I'll have to do is tell it to reveal itself to me, and the front door will always be open when I come to call." He sneered. "But first, you."

"What about me?" Aisling said.

"Ah, yes. What about you," Tiran snorted. "Well, there's not much, is there? You're the seer who didn't see me coming. You're the guardian who couldn't protect. But I suppose we could say you have been most inspiring. Two out of three isn't bad, Aisling. If eejits like you and Jake are the ones keeping the world on track, it's not as if you're doing all that great a job. No wonder I was inspired to take over."

"You'll be a tyrant."

"At least I'll do a better job. No more destinies. No more rules. Everyone will be free to be anything they want. As long as I want them to."

"I'm going to stop you."

"Yes, you're doing a fine job so far."

Tiran held the necklace above the relics. Its gold chain dangled over Tiran's hand. In his palm, the blue-green jade pendant began to glow. "It still doesn't like me," Tiran said. "But that's fine, as long as it does what I want."

Aisling stared. *Grandmother*, she thought, *help me. I don't know what to do now.*

The ends of the pendant's chain glowed bright orange. Then they began to smoke.

"You were right about one thing," Tiran said. "The relics on their own are meaningless. Even here. They have power, sure, but the point of all this isn't to unlock that power. That's just a matter of having the wrong key. Now I have the right one. With the power of the pendant, I will unlock the power of the relics. From there, all the world, all existence is mine."

The chain shortened as the ends of the chain burned and melted like a fuse. *Once there's no more chain*, thought Aisling, *there'll be no more anything.*

As Aisling ran forward, the strangest, biggest grin spread across her face.

Some distant part of her mind remembered the old heroes of Irish legend—how war saw them at their merriest, how it was said their bodies changed, taking on a form of power, rage, and glee.

Tiran faced her. His eyes narrowed and his mouth opened, as if to say no.

Her hand swept over the block and picked up the stick. There was no thought, no aim. She pulled, twirled, moved. The stick blurred and the hand holding the pendant cracked against the block. The pendant flew off to one side, but in the gloom of the chamber floor Aisling couldn't tell where it landed.

Tiran yelled and started to move toward her. He reached for her throat, rage spilling from his voice as he shouted, "You will not stop me!"

Aisling stared at him for a moment. The stick was coming around, but he'd get to her before she could hit him.

Aisling raised her other hand and poked him in the eye.

Tiran doubled over, hands rising to his face.

The stick twirled. Aisling cracked Tiran over the back of the head, and he crashed to the floor.

Aisling dashed past Tiran and dropped to the floor. The stick rolled out of sight, but all that mattered now was finding the pendant. Aisling reached out, sweeping, grabbing, but finding nothing. Then her mind blazed clear, and she could see into the shadows as if the blackness had become brightly lit.

A cry came from behind her. The scrambling noise must have been Tiran rising, but that didn't matter. A sharp and pointed stalagmite, coming up to her waist, rose nearby. She swept her hands all around the floor beneath it. In the shadows something glittered.

As Aisling wrapped her hand around the small pendant, warmth rushed through her like fire, sunlight, and laughter.

Then she was rising.

Tiran's arms tightened under her as he raised her high, aiming her body so the point of the stalagmite would puncture her heart.

Aisling gripped the pendant more tightly. *I could use it, but only to kill. And I could kill him. Destroy him, his twisted plans, his mangled soul.*

The pendant grew warmer in her hand, then hot enough to sear and burn. As she rose, Aisling saw Tiran clearly in her mind. *His own actions would have made him part of The Warning,* she thought, *but now things have changed. I won't kill him. He would use the pendant to harm and enslave, but the pendant doesn't want to be used the way Tiran wants to use it. There has to be another way.*

The pendant's heat faded. A voice entered her mind and said, "Take the power. Because you do not mean to use it, the power offers itself to you freely. Take it. Absorb it."

If I absorb the power of the pendant, Aisling thought, *it dies with me. If the power dies with me, he can do nothing more to the world.*

Tiran stopped moving forward, and he raised her higher.

I wanted to live, Aisling thought. *I did hope for a long life, for love, for the chance to grow old. I wanted to tell stories to a young girl who had the world in her eyes and a future that only I knew. But I am the Awen of*

Ireland, and this is the test. When there is no guide, when I stand alone, hurt, betrayed, with death before and behind, I do what must be done.

Come to me, power of the world. Die with me and we will see what life comes next.

Tiran lowered his arms. Aisling fell.

The feeling of warmth grew, as the pendant in her hand cooled.

Aisling closed her eyes. *Maybe it won't hurt much.*

Then came a cry and an impact. The world jostled. She heard a muffled *oomph.*

The warmth left her. The falling was gone. Tiran's arms were no longer under her, but someone's arms were.

Aisling opened her eyes.

Jay smiled at her. "All right there, Aisling?" he said. The fire of life itself seemed to blaze in his green-gold eyes.

She smiled back. "Yes."

"Thanks for the stick," Jay said. He set her down and she stood next to him. Across from them, Tiran stood doubled over, gripping his crotch.

He looked up.

Jay pointed the stick. "From the moment we met, you felt like a brother to me," he said. "We were friends. Now you've killed that. You're nuts, mate. But it ends here."

"It never ends," Tiran replied, taking a step forward.

Aisling gripped Jay's hand.

"What are you doing?" Jay said to her. "Not that I mind, understand, but this may not be the best time."

The strength flowing through Jay isn't just his own, Aisling thought. *I understand. It all starts here.* She saw it all. She saw the sign and far, far away she saw a city of ash, a smile like flame, a destiny big as the world. "I can't stop him on my own," Aisling replied. She gripped the pendant tightly. "But together, we both can."

"I'll ruin you both," Tiran said. "Rip your bodies into crumbs while you beg to die, while you watch each other die."

Jay gripped Aisling's hand. "What do I do?"

She nodded toward the stick, which still pointed at Tiran. "Keep a steady hand."

With a roar, Tiran leaped.

"I am the muse," Aisling said. "I inspire others to act. The power is not mine to use, but it can pass through me to one who can use it."

A river of lightning flowed through Aisling from the pendant in her hand.

Jay shouted but kept a steady hand.

Silver-gold light erupted from the stick. Strands thick as honey and bright as sunlight wrapped around Tiran, stopping him in midair. His roar cut off as if with a knife, and a panic rose in his frozen eyes.

The light wrapped around him, thicker and thicker, as if it were becoming a cocoon. Soon, Aisling couldn't see Tiran anymore. The warm flow of power faded from her, and the last of the light poured out of the stick. The blazing silver-white light around Tiran pulsed and then grew fainter until all that was left was Tiran, still, eyes closed.

He drifted to the ground like a leaf and lay on the chamber floor unmoving.

Next to her, the fire went out of Jay's eyes, which closed as he fell hard and hit the floor with a smack.

IV

STILL HANGING ON to the pendant, Aisling kneeled by Jay. She touched his face, and his ragged breathing slowed. It became more even but his eyes stayed shut, as if he were sleeping.

"It's a lot for you at this point," she said, looking both at him and at a future far, far away. "But one day, it won't be." She squeezed his hand. "You saved me," she said, "and you saved me again. You were there." She kneeled low and softly kissed him.

Aisling rose and went to Tiran. She checked his pulse as well, even though she knew the answer.

She set the stick on the block, next to the goblet and the box. Movement caught her eye and she went over to Jake. He sat up, breathed in deeply, and then looked at Aisling. "What happened to Tiran and Jay?"

"Jay and I were able to stop Tiran," she replied. "With this." She opened her hand and they stared at the small pendant, still warm as its glow faded.

"That was lost long ago," Jake said. "Tiran had it?"

"Yes," Aisling replied, "but it didn't exactly work the way he expected."

Jake stared at her. "Is Tiran dead?"

"We didn't come here to kill him," Aisling replied. "Not like that. There's no blood on our hands. But we stopped him. For now, that will have to do. The pendant... helped us. It didn't want its power used the way Tiran wanted to use it, and it knew I didn't want to use its power for myself. So it flowed through me, through Jay, and through the stick, blasting Tiran with this strange light. It's like... it's like it *paused* Tiran somehow. He breathes. He's alive but he doesn't really feel... *here*."

Jake walked over to Tiran.

"What do we do with him now?" Aisling asked.

"I'm going to take him to The Management," Jake said. "He is cut off from destiny, and he exists only in decision. Right now, you could say he's not truly in the world. In more ways than one, they may be able to help him."

Aisling looked from Jake to the block. "You're

going to take the relics to them too," she said.

"What are you talking about?"

"The ruse has been a useful deterrent, a useful trap, but its purpose is no more," Aisling replied. "Tiran is like nothing we've ever faced. He mastered the relics, drew powers out of them we've never seen. If the world has changed so that something like him can exist, then the ruse is over. The relics are no longer safe here. They must go with you."

"I'll give them to The Management for safekeeping," Jake replied. "But you should know, if their heir seeks to claim the relics they will be waiting."

"Heir?" Aisling said.

"Yes," he replied. "There is one who could claim them and wield them truly, should decision and destiny so converge. If that one comes, they will be ready." Jake stared at the relics. They faded and then were gone.

"Did you and The Management know this was going to happen?" Aisling asked. *They steer the world,* she thought. *We steer the living but one way or another they set the course.*

Jake sighed. "When it comes to Declan or Tiran, as he's calling himself now, we don't know anything until it happens. The Management suspected he was approaching Ireland, but we did not know the outcome."

"You were testing me and Jay," she said.

Again, silence. "You have to understand," Jake said, "while yes, you were chosen long ago to be Awen, there are some things that a choice and an oath can't decide."

Aisling nodded. "Some things can only be determined by trial."

"If you're angry..."

"I'm not angry," she said. "I understand. If I were you, I would have made the same decisions. But tell me, Jake Connemara, did I pass?"

"The new authority in your voice was really suiting you," Jake replied. "Why do you sound unsure now? Do you really need me to answer?"

Aisling thought. "I made mistakes. I was misled. I let myself be blinded."

"But you gave all," Jake said. "You inspired another to help you. You refused power in favor of a greater purpose. You were ready to die to save the world. I think it's safe to say that in the end you passed." He smiled. "Tiran is like nothing we've seen before. Lucky for us, so are you. You made good, Awen of Ireland. Your grandmother would be proud."

"What of Jay? There's something much bigger at stake for him, I know. That's why he can't stay."

"I don't really know either," Jake said. "I know his path goes on, but that's it."

"He was never going to stay here," Aisling said.

"From what little The Management told me, that

is preferable for the world's longevity."

"What happens when he wakes?"

Jake kneeled by Jay and took a flask from his pocket. "He wakes," Jake said, pouring a thin amber liquid into Jay's mouth. "I'll be gone and he won't remember what actually happened. He's a long way to go before he's really ready."

"Won't remember?" said Aisling. "Did the intensity of the experience wipe away his memory, or are you doing that for him?"

"A bit of both," Jake replied, standing and putting the flask back into his pocket.

"I suppose I'll tell him we did a bit of caving, will I?" Aisling said. "He hit his head?"

"That's what I would've suggested."

She sighed.

"You seem sad all of a sudden, Awen," Jake said. "Remember, we won. The world's still going the way it should be."

"For a moment, he was similar to me," Aisling replied. "A purpose larger than himself loomed in front of him, and he moved toward it with open eyes. Now he'll just be a simple traveler again."

"Part of you hoped for something... more."

She nodded. "I wondered. But now he just has to leave."

"That's true. Jay will leave," Jake said, smiling. "But it doesn't mean he has to leave right away."

Aisling smiled back. "Good point."

"He's going to wake soon," Jake said. "I'd better go."

"Before you do," Aisling said, "there's one more thing."

"What?"

Aisling opened her hand. The gold pendant gleamed, and the green and blue tones of the jade seemed to pulse like a heartbeat.

"This is more powerful than the relics," Aisling said. "It should go with you too."

Something caught Jake's eye. He moved toward the mouth of the chamber, reached down, and came up holding the jagged remnants of the knotted necklace.

"Jay gave me that," Aisling said. "I can't believe you found it. She held out her hand.

Jake didn't move. "The Renewal," he said distantly as he stared at the necklace.

"Well, yeah," said Aisling. "But he just found it in some shop, he told me."

"Oh, you can find things in the pattern all over the place nowadays. Sure," Jake said. "But you can't find this piece just anywhere." He held it up. "This isn't just The Renewal. This is... Well, this is *The Renewal*. The original."

"What?"

Jake grinned. "Just as your grandmother designed it too. I'd love to know which shop Jay found it in..."

Aisling stared at the necklace. "I never knew."

"This is yours," Jake said, "but it's been damaged. May I take it with me? If anyone can repair it properly, The Management can."

Aisling stared at the necklace, and a longing filled her. *So many things I still don't know*, she thought. *Even about you, Grandmother. What else is the Awen going to learn about the Awen?*

She nodded. "Take it, please. And send The Management my thanks."

Jake tucked the necklace and the pendant into his pockets.

"This won't be the end of tests and battles," Aisling said. "Will it?"

"No, it won't," Jake replied. "But should you see him again, you'll be even better prepared."

"What do you mean?"

Jake stood next to Tiran. "I mean that we will try," Jake said, "but with Tiran, nothing is certain. Good luck." Jake winked. "See you down the pub soon."

They faded, leaving Aisling and Jay alone in the cave.

"I passed," Aisling said. "I protected. I did better than I thought, I suppose. But yes, there'll be a next time. And I will be ready."

Beside her, Jay stirred and opened his eyes.

Aisling smiled. "That was quite a slip and a knock on the head," she said as he got to his feet. "Care to keep going deeper into this cave, or are you ready to turn around?"

Jay shook his head. "Oy," he said. "Only thing I'm ready for is a beer. Let's head back."

They wandered through the passage, back through the large cavern, and toward the cave entrance. Outside, the clouds had cleared and the stars were lighting up the darkness. They said little as they walked to the hostel.

"It's been a great evening," Jay said at the door. "I'd better be off, though. Need to figure out somewhere to stay tonight."

"You're in luck," Aisling said, squeezing his hand. "I do believe a bed just opened up."

AISLING STOOD OUTSIDE the hostel, staring at the walls of the new kitchen. Progress over the past month had been fast, and she was relieved to have a proper kitchen again. The contractor had even taken a strange hollow space in the floor and made it into a handy little storage area.

A growing local thirst had helped the work on the pub go even faster than the hostel kitchen. Jake said they would reopen that night.

The front door opened, and Jay came out, carrying two steaming mugs. "Another day, another coffee," he said. "You'd better be careful, Aisling. You may have converted."

She smiled as she accepted the mug, grateful for

the warmth on her cool hands. A slight breeze ran up her dressing gown and the brown T-shirt beneath it. "We'll have to see," she said with a shiver. "You may be incapable of a drinkable cuppa tea, but you make up for it with your coffee." She winked. "Well, amongst other things."

They stared at each other. Then their smiles faded and they looked away.

With time the bumps and scratches had faded too. There had been no sign of any other trouble. Tiran was with The Management, whatever that would mean. Though Jake never mentioned what was happening between Aisling and Jay, he always kept his mouth shut with the teeniest smile. Aisling looked past the hostel to the hills rising in the east. The mountain still stood.

And the mountain still glowered. Sometimes Aisling wondered if it was getting impatient with the globetrotter who was currently staying put. *Approve or disapprove,* Aisling thought, *Jay and I had shared the world. Conversations, kisses, nights that seemed never to end or that never should.*

But it's all ending now.

"Aisling?" Jay put his arm around her waist. "Lost in your thoughts?"

"I always find my way back."

"So what does today hold?"

She touched his face. "A send-off," she said.

"Oh? For who?"

She kissed him. "For you."

"Aisling…"

"You know it as well as I do. I can see it in your face. The way your eyes linger when you look at your backpack. The way you dream. The things you don't say."

"You know I love being here. With you."

"I know. That's not the point. Someday, if you ever truly tire of the road, well, we could see then." She looked at Jay and touched his face. "After a fashion, you did get to make Clifden home for a while. Call it a respite. Call it thanks. You'll wonder every day what else could be between us—what sort of life you could have here. But your feet long for your boots, and your back longs for that heavy-arse pack of yours. You want my heart, but you need the road."

Jay looked away, but Aisling saw the wet glint in his eyes. "I know you're right," he said. "I love it here. I love being with you. But there's more I need to see of the world. I have to be out there. The road is the only home I know now." He looked at her again and took her hand. "I wish I could stay. I wish I could want to stay as much as I need to go."

"I'll miss you more than anything," Aisling said, "but I understand. You have a world to travel and must be on your way." She squeezed his hand and pulled him close. "You will always have a place here, Jay, and someone who trusts you and someone you can trust. But you know what?"

"What?"

"Not quite yet. One more day."

He nodded. "Okay. One more day. One last day."

They drank their coffees in silence. While the hot liquid should have warmed her, Aisling still just felt cold.

As they went through the morning, she could feel little distances grow between them. She did extra cleaning in another part of the hostel, knowing that all the while Jay was prepping his backpack, making sure everything was packed and ready.

We have one last day, Aisling thought. *Then maybe we could have another one tomorrow and another one after that. What if we treated every day as a last day?*

But even as she thought it, Aisling knew it would never happen. Standing at a window that faced the hills and the mountain, Aisling thought, *I've had a break, just like Jay. A chance to recharge. Maybe a reward. There will always be something between us. I know he has to leave tomorrow, but as for the tomorrows after that, I don't know any more than the mountain does.*

I only know there is much to do, and I do what must be done.

Aisling went back toward her room. Jay was kneeling by his pack, zipping it closed.

"We're going to the pub tonight," Aisling said. "You'll have a proper send-off. I know that in the end, Clifden isn't home. But it's come to like you a lot. I have a feeling you won't be buying many pints."

"Will you play your fiddle?"

"Oh," she said with a smile. "I'll do more than that."

AS THE DAY WOUND on toward afternoon and evening, Jay and Aisling sat in the hostel, drinking endless coffees and talking. They talked as if they had first met; they talked as if they would never see each other again. In the evening, after a well-earned nap, they wandered toward The Salt and Crane.

"Weird," Jay said as they passed an empty shop front. "It was here."

"What was?"

"An old man ran the place. It was the shop where I bought you that necklace—the one that got lost when I fell in the cave."

Aisling stared at the dusty glass windows. *Who were you?* she thought. *The Awen will find out. But not today.*

Jake was standing outside when they came to the door. "I'd hoped you two would be the first," Jake said, shaking Jay's hand and giving Aisling a hug. He unlocked the door. "We just finished polishing everything. Come on in. Two pints of GPS coming right up. On the house."

Jake had hardly started pouring their pints when other people began wandering in. Soon the pub was packed, as if half of Western Ireland had turned out for the return of The Salt and Crane.

Aisling drank some of her pint and then kissed Jay on the cheek. "Every song I play tonight," she said, "I play for you."

She set her beer and fiddle in the back corner of the room. Instead of sitting down to play, Aisling stood straight. The room went quiet. *There's a time I would've wondered if the respect was for me or for the Awen,* she thought. *Now I understand: there is no difference.*

"It's said there's no rest for the wandering," Aisling said. "But there are good times to be had for the wandering, during wee pauses between heres and theres. Over the past weeks, while he's paused here, you've gotten to know Jay."

Cheers went up in the pub. "Yes, yes," she said, "the least annoying Annoyican ever." She winked at Jay as people laughed. "Tomorrow, Jay will be leaving us. The road is his home and his home is the road. But for a bit, he wondered, could this be home?" She shook her head. "As much as we can praise his taste, no, I'm afraid not. It's true, Jay, you won't be calling Clifden home." She smiled. "But you can always call us friends."

Cheers and applause rose. When all was quiet again, Aisling began to sing, and her voice was the only sound in the pub.

Grandmother had taught her the old tune as a girl, and to Aisling it had always sounded both ancient and brand new. Versatility made it everlasting, Grandmother had said. The tune was so enduring because it was so flexible. It could be adapted to any instrument. It could be matched to any words worthy of the tune. It had no name; you either knew how it went, or you wished you did.

Aisling thought of the mountain and of Jay, of all that had happened, of all that was to come for him, for her, for the world. As she thought, she faded into what she saw, and as she sang, the words appeared in her heart and wrote themselves into the tune:

> A footstep song calls us away,
> Smaller than the world, more than home;
> Our hearts go, even if our love stays,
> Blood runs, breezes blow, we ever roam.
>
> Life is so short. Life is so long.
> The cracked earth glitters where we strode;
> Home sweet home will never be our song.
> Live the world, we sing, home sweet road.

She sang it again and again and again, as the people cried for more. When at last she sat down and took up her fiddle, nodding thanks to the pints that had begun appearing, she couldn't help but feel a little sad. *To be the Awen is to say only what must be said,* she thought, *and then to know when to shut up.*

I won't sing the third verse here.

Jay danced with half the women in the pub. When he wasn't dancing, he was talking with everyone, and every hand in Clifden slapped him on the back. Aisling transitioned the music from "Wizard Walk" to "The White Sign," and then to "The Traveler."

As she and Jay and the rest of Clifden finally staggered out of the pub, the night lay heavy and deep on the world. "What time is it?" Jay said.

"Whatever it is," Aisling replied, "it's too close to dawn to be to my liking." She put her hands in her pockets. Her right hand brushed a small packet that hadn't been there before. Aisling's memory jumped to Jake's hug.

Jay stopped. "I'm going to miss you and Clifden more than I've ever missed anyone or anywhere," he said.

"I know," Aisling replied, taking his hand. "But the world is round, Jay of the road. Who knows? It just may turn you back here someday. I do know this, though: no matter how far you go, I'll always be near."

They wandered back to the hostel. Inside, confusion covered Jay's face. "Maybe I should stay in the dorm tonight, Aisling," he said.

"You'll do no such thing."

"I don't want to make this harder than it already is."

"Oh, you're going to leave." Aisling kissed him. "We both know it. But you're not leaving yet." She pressed her body to his. "Clifden gave you its send-off," she said. "Now I'm going to give you mine."

The sun was high when at last they got out of bed. Together they made an Irish breakfast, with both coffee and tea. Afterward, Jay got his backpack from the dorm room.

"Sure you can manage it?" Aisling asked.

With one fluid motion, Jay settled the pack on his back and tightened the shoulder, chest, and hip straps around him. "I hardly know it's there, but I know it's always there. It's like my best friend, you know?" He smiled at Aisling. "Thanks for helping me get back on the road."

She squeezed his hand. "I'll go with you to the edge of town."

"How did you know?"

"That you didn't want to catch the bus from the city center, but only once you'd walked a ways?" She shook her head. "Anything else just wouldn't be you. Besides, you won't feel like you're leaving until you've stood at the sign one last time, am I right?"

They walked with a full sun and a blue sky above them. The night's music and revels had long passed, but the air still shimmered with the fading sounds of fiddles and laughter, with clinking glasses and songs being sung. Jay and Aisling said nothing; they just felt the road under their feet. They felt the nearness of each other, and they kept going.

When they stood at the sign, Jay smiled. "Sometimes," he said, "I swear it winks at me."

A new arrow pointed southeast. "Lhasa, Tibet," said the sign. "7,166 km/4,453 miles." And beneath that, another sign said, "Agamuskara, India. 8,225 km/5,111 miles."

"Tibet and then India," Jay said, smiling. He stuck his thumbs under his padded shoulder straps. "That sounds like an excellent idea." Aisling hugged him. They hung that way awhile, arms and unsaid thoughts entwined. Jay stepped back. "Another time," he said.

She nodded. "Another time, traveler. Enjoy the road, Jay. I'll be seeing you."

Aisling stood by the sign, watching as Jay started traveling toward Asia.

He'd only walked a little ways when he looked back, smiling at Aisling. "I guess you were right," he called to her. "There are only twelve."

She turned to look behind her. The warm sun shone on the Twelve Bens, but only them. The mountain had made the Twelve Bens look like teacups, the Himalayas like wee hills, but when Jay left Clifden, the mountain left too.

Turning again, Jay was already out of sight. She

imagined him walking, farther from Clifden, closer to Asia. *He will keep wandering,* Aisling thought, *and I will keep staying here.* She reached into her pocket, then took out the small packet and opened it.

The necklace had been restored. Silver shone like moonlight, and a dark blackish-brown metal threaded through the silver like woven shadow. Where the pattern had simply been interesting and beautiful, now it was as if the very fabric of life and existence flowed through the knotwork. Attached to the center of the necklace, the pendant's gold gleamed like the sun. The blues and greens of the jade glinted.

The Management hadn't just fixed the necklace; they had combined it with the pendant.

A note lay underneath. "The ruse is over. Harder challenges lay before you now," she read. "Something this powerful can help you inspire like never before. Something this powerful is safe with someone who doesn't want to use power but who combines love and power the way you do. There is no better place. There is no better protector. Accept it, Awen of Ireland, with our thanks."

It was signed, simply, "The Management."

Aisling put on the necklace. Warmth flowed through her, soft as a summer breeze, warm as a winter fire. The voice came back. "The Awen does," it said. "The Awen remains. The Awen is always."

When she looked up, the white sign changed.

The arrows disappeared, leaving the post bare. Even the CLIFDEN lettering faded. On top of the post, a small globe slowly turned. *The detail is exquisite,* Aisling thought. *You can even see clouds moving. It's like it's our own world...*

As Aisling watched the small globe turn, it was as if she could see all that lay before Jay on his road, on his endless, endless road. Then she was back in Ireland, to the previous night in The Salt and Crane. Aisling sang the song again.

> A footstep song calls us away,
> Smaller than the world, more than home;
> Our hearts go, even if our love stays,
> Blood runs, breezes blow, we ever roam.
>
> Life is so short. Life is so long.
> The cracked earth glitters where we strode;
> Home sweet home will never be our song.
> Live the world, we sing, home sweet road.

Her voice moved soft and low over the two verses, and she added the mountain's gift, the third, final verse, as the mountain had sung it to her:

> Before mountainrise, mountainfall,
> Just as life's final footsteps fade;
> A river stops the breath of us all,
> Yet old black dies to blue and jade.

THANK YOU FOR READING!

Please tell your friends about this story and review it at your favorite bookstore. Reviews are the best way readers discover great new books, and I would truly appreciate it. Even a couple of sentences is a big help. Here's a list of stores:

anthonystclair.com/homesweetroad

MORE FROM THE RUCKSACK UNIVERSE

The Martini of Destiny
anthonystclair.com/martini

Forever the Road
anthonystclair.com/forevertheroad

SUBSCRIBE TODAY

New story announcements, events, exclusive bonuses and more. Join the free email list:

anthonystclair.com/subscribe

In 2000, I had the joy of living in Ireland for a few months. My thanks to all the people I met along the way in Dublin, Galway, the Aran Islands, Clifden, and more. Also, thanks to Guinness, Murphys, and Beamish for making stout part of my soul.

To my wonderful Beta Readers, your insights always save the day. Bonnie Donaghy, there are exciting times ahead. And thank you, Scott Jones, for polishing the rough edges of this story.

Jodie, thank you for believing in me. And Connor, thank you for keeping me true to myself and for being a ridiculously cute toddler.

ABOUT THE AUTHOR

Globetrotter, homebrewer and writer Anthony St. Clair has walked with hairy coos in the Scottish Highlands, choked on seafood in Australia, and watched the full moon rise over Mt. Everest in Tibet. Anthony's travels have also taken him around the sights and beers of Thailand, Japan, India, Canada, Ireland, the USA, Cambodia, China and Nepal. He and his wife live in Oregon and gave their son a passport for his first birthday. Learn more and connect:

www.anthonystclair.com